I0769146

Cover art by Daniel Thiede.
Map art by Nate Baldwin.

*For the Relic "stunt doubles" -- Doug Donato,
Ron Kopriva, Buck Tilton, Ron Smith*

And for Walt Gaub and Don Mead

*And for all the great folks who worked at
Wind River Legal Services*

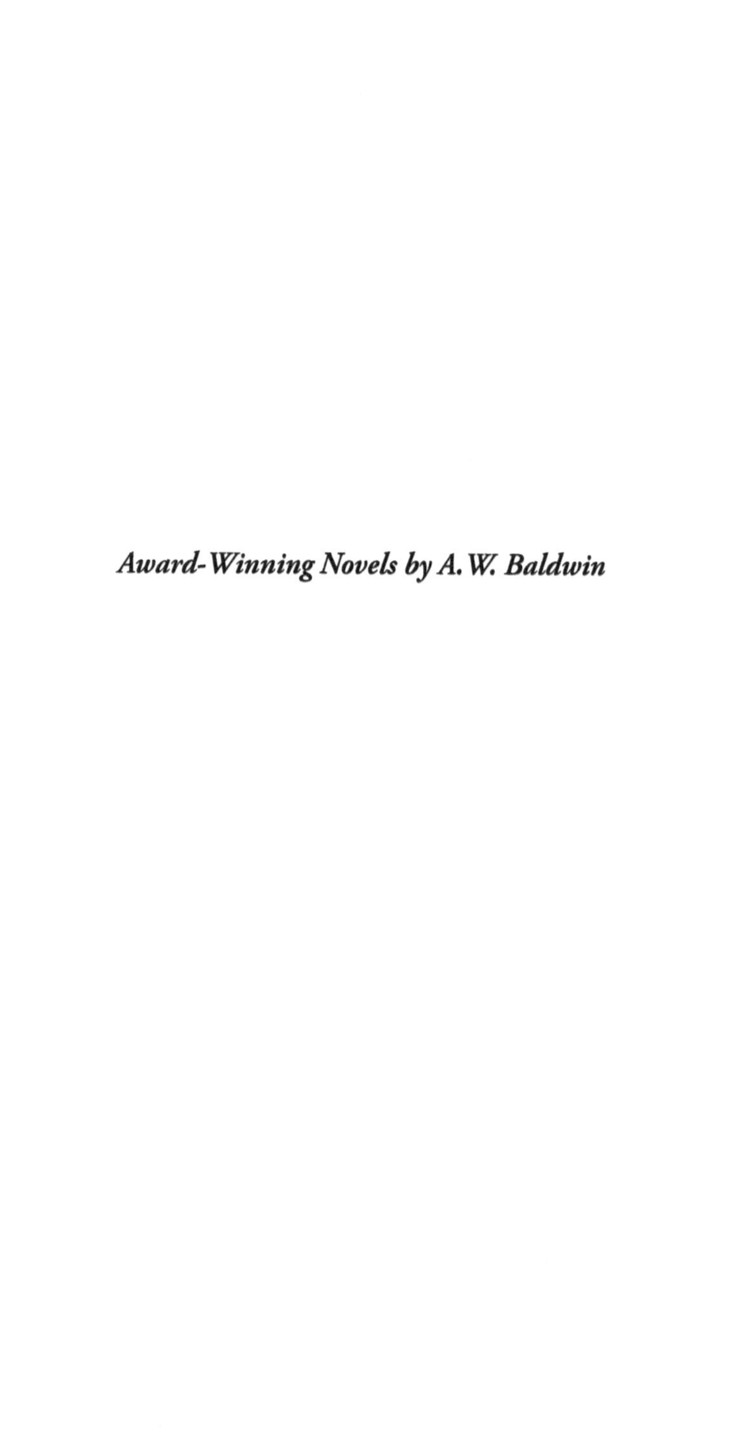

Award-Winning Novels by A. W. Baldwin

SLICKROCK

Murder at ancient ruins, desperate kidnappers, and a $5 million-dollar ransom make Slickrock Canyon a deadly place for a finance student, an intrepid deputy, and a moonshining hermit.

"a brilliant plot… with a fantastic climax" Slickrock "is sure to please and impossible to put down. Very highly recommended."
> — *Readers' Favorite*

"Take a desert hermit to rival Hiaasen's brilliantly eccentric Skink, throw in a dash of Hillerman's reverence for Native American cultures, and pour a stiff shot of Cussler. Shake vigorously until the mixture explodes. into another mind-blowing A.W. Baldwin adventure."
> — *Jeff Edwards, Bestselling Author of Steel Wind and Darwin's Razor.*

"Slickrock is action married to ethics, justice tempered with wonder. Loved it!"
> — *Award winning author Sarah Blanchard*
> *(Drawn from Life, Grabtown)*

AGAINST THE WIND

The skies are a dangerous place for a teenage pilot with a stolen airplane and a physicist with a quantum computer secret.

"This entertaining thriller will have you hooked from start to finish with its upbeat tempo that never let's go…. The writing was absolutely stunning…Two people from different backgrounds with different goals are brought together on a treacherous journey to an unknown destination."

"…a powerful reminder of the positive impact that human relationships can have on our lives.…a page-turner and a must-read for anyone who enjoys thrilling adventure novels with memorable characters."

"An exhilarating adventure from the opening salvo, Against the Wind follows a global race for next-generation quantum computing technology replete with hitmen, spies, scientists, and a headstrong runaway orphan suddenly thrust into the center of a global threat to national security."

Bronze Medal Winner Global Book Awards, Distinguished Favorite, Independent Press Award and New York City Big Book Award, Readers' Favorite Five Star review.

MOONSHINE MESA

Criminal clients, a pollution mitigation scam, and a million-dollar double-cross make Moonshine Mesa a dangerous place for an aspiring lawyer, an intrepid deputy, and a moonshining hermit.

"witty dialogue and humor…[with] vibrant characters whose personalities leap off the pages"

"…a sleuth murder mystery, crime-drama thriller, and action novel all rolled into one page-turner"

"…a fascinating dynamic… If you enjoy crime capers, dry humor, and quirky characters, you won't go wrong with Moonshine Mesa."
— Readers' Favorite Five Star Reviews.

First Place Gold Medal Winner of Readers' Favorite Book Award, Gold Medal Winner Global Book Awards, and Gold Medal Winner Literary Titan Award.

THE ANTIDOTE

Can a botany student, a couple of old-timers, and genetically modified seeds provide the antidote for climate change? The cross-hairs on those million-dollar seeds are on them, too…

"A rollicking cross-country chase to save the planet… Captivating heroes, murderous threats…and a classic Chevy Bel Air star in this exciting thriller that will make you want to hop in and hit the gas."
 — *#1 New York Times Best-selling author Dirk Cussler.*

"The chemistry between Harry and Keaton is electrifying."
"…there is never a dull moment…The Antidote [is] a gripping novel."
 — *Readers' Favorite 5 Star Reviews.*

First Place winner of the Grand Master Adventure Writer's Award, Finalist Award from ScreenCraft Cinematic Book Competition, and awards from Global Book Awards, Literary Titan, and Wishing Shelf competitions.

BROKEN INN

The mob, undercover agents, and secret payloads make Broken Inn a dangerous place for a fresh reporter, a newspaper photographer, and a moonshining hermit.

"The desert bakes while the danger scorches in another outstanding mystery from A.W. Baldwin."
> — *#1 New York Times Bestselling Author Dirk Cussler.*

Winner of awards from the Grand Master Adventure Writer's Competition, New York City Big Book Awards, Independent Press Awards, Global Book Awards, and Books Shelf Writing Awards.

WINGS OVER GHOST CREEK

Can a moonshining hermit, a reluctant pilot, and a misfit student uncover the truth and escape an archeology field class that hides assassins and dealers in black-market treasure?

Baldwin has a "gift for capturing the reader's attention at the beginning and keeping them spellbound."
— ***Onlinebookclub.org review***

Winner of awards from the Grand Master Adventure Writer's Competition and Global Book Awards; Reader's Favorite Five Star Review.

RAPTOR CANYON

Armed with a full box of toothpicks (and a little dynamite), can a moonshining hermit, a big-city lawyer, and a student with secret ties to the site monkey-wrench a corrupt land deal and recast the fate of Raptor Canyon?

"A gem of a read…"

> *— #1 New York Times best-selling author*
> *Dirk Cussler*

"[You'll be] holding your heart and your breath at the same time…"

> *— Peter Greene, award winning author of The*
> *Adventures of Jonathan Moore series*

"A hoot of an adventure novel…"

> *— - Reader's Favorite.*

Grand Master Adventure Writer's Finalist Award and Screencraft Cinematic Book Contest Semi-finalist; Reader's Favorite Five Star Review.

DIAMONDS OF DEVIL'S TAIL

When diamonds appear in a remote canyon stream, whitewater rafters and artifact thieves set off in a deadly race to the source.

"*Relic* is a unique and intriguing character…passionately interested in preserving the ancient archeological sites and conserving the land and water…[We] enthusiastically recommend it to readers who enjoy thrillers, action-packed adventure, and crime novels."
    – Onlinebookclub.org four out of four Star Review.

"Another rollicking Relic ride from A.W. Baldwin…a bunch of double-crossing, dirt dealing, diamond thieves run into Relic's trademark wit and ingenuity. Enjoy!"
    – Jacob P. Avila, Cave Diver.

"…an adeptly written thriller…the excitement and tension are superb…the
entire plot [is] compelling"
    – Readers' Favorite Five Star Review.

DESERT GUARDIAN

A moonshining hermit; a campus bookworm; a midnight murder. Can an unlikely duo and a whitewater crew save themselves and an ancient Aztec battlefield from deadly looters?

Desert Guardian is an "engaging action… mystery" with "tough, credible characters."
    – *Readers' Favorite Five Star Review.*

Buy now from a bookstore near you or amazon.com
For more about these award-winning books go to:
AWBALDWIN.COM

A.W. BALDWIN

SLICK ROCK

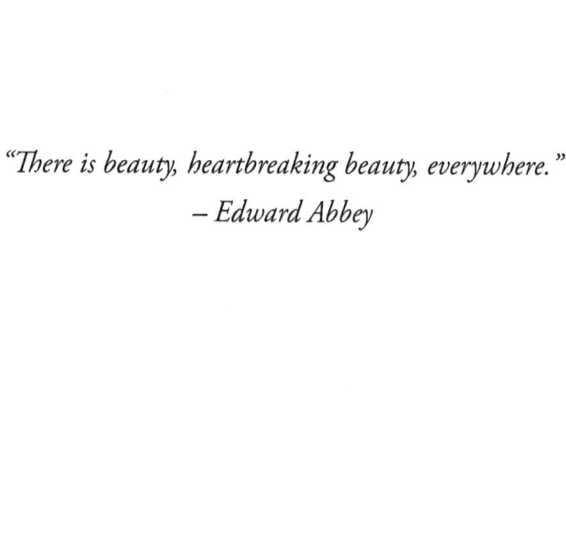

"There is beauty, heartbreaking beauty, everywhere."
– Edward Abbey

Slick Rock Canyon
Arroyo
Limestone shelf
Box canyon
Slot canyon

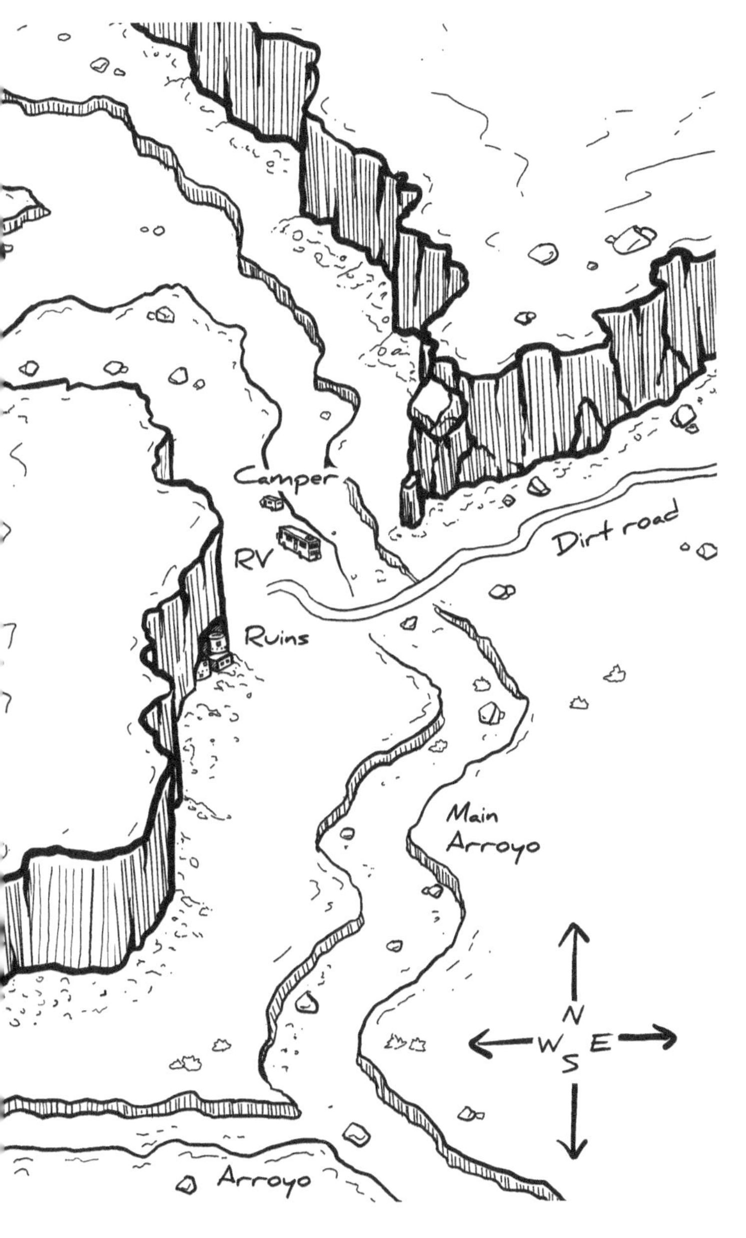

Camper
RV
Ruins
Dirt road
Main
Arroyo
Arroyo
N
W E
S

CHAPTER 1

"It seems like the more things change, the more they stay insane."

Relic smoothed his dark goatee and adjusted the compact binoculars to his eyes. Cottonwood leaves clattered in the breeze, the rise and fall of distant applause. Across the arroyo, sheer, red-rock cliffs rose to the polished sky.

A part-time moonshiner and full-time wanderer, these canyons, flats, and hoodoos were Relic's home. An eclectic mixture of Scottish and Hopi, he traded his hooch for what little he needed from civilization and otherwise lived off the land, as the white man would say, leaving no trace but for caches of water and a couple of antiquated stills tucked into hidden crags.

A hundred yards away, a man in a dirty T-shirt and jeans stacked brick-sized chunks of red sandstone into a semi-circle at the base of an overhang. Cliffs rose along either side of him, towering eight hundred feet above, the start of Slickrock Canyon. Around the bend, a place called Star Chart Ruins meandered along the outcrop, a row of stone and mortar apartments, storage granaries, and celestial markers built by ancestral pueblo people a thousand years ago. Vacant doors stared into the canyon like missing teeth in a crooked smile.

If they weren't in the middle of nowhere, they sure as hell could see the place from here.

Star Chart Ruins earned its name when archeologists discovered that a series of pecks in the stone coincided with the locations of Venus and a host of stars in the summer sky. The pecks were adjacent to a marker showing the summer solstice—a place where the sun, at its zenith, overlaid an etching in the cliffs. The ancients had studied the cosmos and carved a map of the midnight sky into the bluffs near their homes.

So, what was someone doing now—building a modern-day replica of a stone-age structure? What did that man plan to store in that thing?

A great blue heron, long and lanky, slipped into view, its bony shoulders pumping the air like a pterodactyl.

The man reached into a white bucket at his feet

and spread mud between the stones he'd laid. He stacked another row and capped the structure with a wide, flat stone and stuffed his homemade mortar into the cracks. He turned and looked toward Relic, his cheeks like oven-baked dinner rolls, his eyes like sun-dried raisins. Relic stayed hidden behind the tree trunk.

The man gathered something from the ground and dropped it into the bucket. He brushed off his pants and walked down from the rise where he'd worked and toward the pueblo ruins.

Relic stood and shouldered his pack, waiting until the man was around the bend and fully out of sight. He pulled his ponytail tight against his head and moved toward the new granary, dropping into the dry creek bed and out of it on the other side. He set his pack at the base of the structure and the scent of something rank stopped him cold.

He'd smelled this before.

He reached for the stone lid and pulled it from the top, suction tugging the mortar with it, the sound of muck being drawn through a straw.

Inside, a body curled tightly against itself, skin shrunken against the skull, sharp cheekbones, forehead already mummifying in the desert heat. Its eyes were closed and hollowed, lips shrunk into a snarl, a blue plaid shirt dusty and loose around its shoulders.

CHAPTER 2

Malia hurried from her dormitory room across the slick pavement, campus lights reflecting against the polished black of the waiting Escalade. Cool, autumn air seemed to breathe across her neck, and she wished she'd brought a jacket. Her pant legs brushed against each other with each long stride. She knew she should be studying for a quiz in Intro to Statistics, but her friend Sheila had invited her to a hot, new nightclub, an opportunity Malia was not going to pass up. She hopped inside and closed the door.

"What happened to your little Mazda?" Malia asked.

"In the shop for something." Sheila rolled her eyes and pushed her hair from her forehead. "Got this monster for now."

"Your mom's?"

"Yeah. Hey, I love your top."

"Almost matches yours," Malia glanced at Sheila's

blouse and a white shawl on the seat beside her. She turned to watch the college lights fade into the distance.

"Hey, tonight…" Sheila began. "If I decide to hook up, you can catch a ride back home, right?"

"Sure. Lyft or Uber, if nothing else."

"If nothing else," Sheila's eyes peered from under her brow, her words soaked in inuendo. Malia knew what she meant: if Malia didn't hook up with a date of her own.

Malia wiggled in her seat, not as comfortable with the idea as Sheila, but working on it. She admired the ease with which Sheila seemed to go through life—enjoying the clothes, the money, the attentive young men. Sheila had become a semi-famous blogger and a podcaster who shared her views about popular culture. Sheila's stepfather owned Cordite Hills Mining Company, a mid-size business that hit it big ten years ago with a cache of rare earth minerals, material needed for batteries to operate electric cars and trucks. Malia's father was a public defender, his fortunes limited to thinning government budgets. But he'd also made some money investing in high-value minerals. The girls met each other in a study group for first-year students at City College.

"You're not taking the freeway?" Malia asked.

"Too busy this time of night. I'm going to take a back way, along this park," she nodded ahead of them.

Anemic streetlights on skinny poles lined the road, casting yellow orbs on the manicured grass.

"There's a crosswalk up ahead," Malia pointed.

"Nobody's out here this time of night." Sheila kept her speed steady.

"Yeah, well…"

Sheila changed the subject. "Hey, we've got to see that new show coming to the Delia Theater. You know? The German male dance troupe?"

"Sheila…" Malia nodded toward the front windshield, a reminder to keep her eyes on the road.

"Yes," Sheila blinked, some sort of passive resistance.

"Hey!" Malia yelled.

Something dark brown darted in front of them, left to right, toward the grass of the park.

Thump!

The Escalade shuddered, then spun toward the open ground and bounced hard across the curb. Sheila braked, pulling them to a stop.

"Shit." Malia's hands were tight against the dash.

They looked at each other.

"Hey, the airbags didn't go off," Malia said.

"Not that hard of a hit, I guess." Sheila turned in her seat, searching behind them. "What did we hit?"

"I don't know." Malia unbuckled and slid from the Escalade to the ground. She held her hands to her knees for a moment, then saw what she was looking for: the animal lay motionless in the grass at the edge of light from one of the streetlamps.

Sheila came around the vehicle. "You all right?"

Malia nodded. "Yeah, maybe we hit a deer."

"Stupid thing. Ran right in front of me."

"Look," Malia took a step closer. "It's a baby. A fawn."

"Well, it's dead now." Sheila put her hands on her hips. "Damn thing." She moved to the front of the Escalade. "Made a helluva dent in the bumper."

Malia took another step towards the deer.

"Don't go near that thing," Sheila said. "We don't know what kind of germs or lice or other gunk it carries around."

"It's just a fawn…"

"It's just an animal. And Mom's gonna be pissed when she sees this bumper," Sheila pointed at the dented chrome. "Thank god the headlight's okay. Besides, it's just a dumb animal. Who cares?"

Malia watched the deer for another minute, satisfying herself that it was dead. "Shouldn't we report it, or something?"

"Who to?"

"Parks department? Is there a wildlife department?"

"Hell, no. They'll find it in the morning."

Malia stood there for a moment, still looking at the fawn.

"Come on, we've got to get going. We're okay, the car's okay, and we've got a hot dance floor waiting for us." Sheila ran a hand through her hair and walked across the front of the car, its headlamps flashing against her slacks as she went.

No other sound interrupted the rumbling idle of the engine.

"Yeah, I guess you're right," Malia mumbled to herself. "Just a dumb animal." She climbed into her seat and shut the door.

Sheila backed them slowly out of the park and into the street, slipped into drive, and sped again down the poorly lit road.

CHAPTER 3

Malia touched the gloss to her lips and smacked them together, watching herself in a giant mirror. Paintings of gilded ferns and tiny flowers hung along either side on charcoal-colored walls, the sinks and soap holders made of Carrara marble. Her friend Sheila stood behind her, turning left and right, checking for perfection. They both wore black slacks and dark tops; Sheila's shoulders were draped with a white lace shawl. Malia had her hair cut the day before in a style similar to Sheila's, a stylish Italian bob, just above her shoulders.

Malia stared into her own eyes for a moment, the sensation disquieting. Her sister, Anne, had those same eyes. She was eight years older than Malia and had moved ten months ago to Bangor, Maine, hell and away from Malia's dormitory at Los Angeles City College. They'd been close despite their age difference, California born and bred. But video calls between them had grown less and less frequent over the months, the daily news between them less and less urgent. And now Anne had found a boyfriend, a handsome civil engineer who took much of her time and energy. Some of Sheila's way of speaking reminded her of Anne, at least a little bit, and hanging out with Sheila had become a sort of substitution, weak tea being better than none. As Malia considered all of this, she wondered, who was that girl gazing back at her?

The floor pounded with the beat of bass drums, voices and high notes muffled behind the bathroom doors. Tonight was "lady's night," with half-priced drinks. Half the outrageous, regular price, she thought.

Sheila had invited her to the Black Spider Lounge, offering to pay the cover charge. It had become a minor tradition for the two girls. A way to celebrate their hard work at college. Or, rather, an excuse to get out and party. Rebuilt after a fire in a posh section of West Hollywood, the lounge featured a live DJ, modern pop music, and plenty of male dance partners. They'd come up to a second-floor balcony of sorts, with a row of tables along a brass railing that overlooked the main floor.

"Ready?" Sheila waved toward the door.

Malia followed Sheila back to the lounge, the heavy metal beat hitting them now like a surge of voltage, tingling her fingers. Or maybe it was those earlier shots of blackberry vodka they'd pre-gamed.

Black lights mounted on the ceiling cast a neon glow on Sheila's cloak. Sheila nodded her head toward two men in the corner, guys they'd noticed watching them earlier, and kept moving toward a table along the railing. Below them hung a massive gold and glass chandelier, gaudy and glistening like it had been dipped in cooking oil. The main bar spread below the huge fixture, a circle of bartenders reaching for bottles, pouring from shaker tins, scurrying liquor to inebriate customers. Flickers and flashes glittered the mezzanine.

Malia sat and watched the mass of humans stomping and gyrating on the dance floor below, some sort of variegated organism squirming on a microscope slide.

"Wanna shot?" Sheila's words drowned in the music, but Malia read her lips.

"Not if I have to pay for it," she smiled.

"Don't you love this place?" Sheila mouthed. "Love getting lost in this world?"

Malia nodded.

The music shifted for a slower dance, the percussion melting into hushed strokes across the drum.

"Those two guys are watching us again," Malia said.

"Let 'em look. If they want to dance, they'll come over." Sheila swayed her shoulders with the music.

"Right."

Tinted reflections bounced off a mirrored ball in the ceiling, splattering colors on the room below them. A musty scent of marijuana wafted through the balcony.

"Hey, there," Sheila spoke to someone who'd come up behind them, so Malia turned to look.

"Wanna dance?" A young man leaned toward them, his ascending smile liquored and lopsided.

"Sure," Sheila stood and slid her purse and shawl from her shoulders. "Keep these for me?" She handed them to Malia.

Sheila and her dance partner walked down the stairs and onto the crowded floor.

Malia wrapped the shawl around her shoulders, luminescent under the black light, and let her mind wander with the soft beat of the music.

A new song gyrated through the air. She leaned her chin in her hand and stared at the distant wall, wondering what her future would be like; whether she would crawl to the top of the human horde or drown beneath it. "Morbid," she told herself. "Stop thinking that way."

"Buy you a drink?" The man's voice startled her from behind, abrupt and tinny. She twisted to her right to see him and felt another presence on her left. Something seemed odd about the man on her right, and he was standing too close to her. She began to say, "No thanks," but the words had barely formed when someone else clamped her left arm tightly against the table and yanked up her sleeve.

"Hey," she twisted her head from right to left and back again, feeling the sting of a needle in her skin. She yanked her arm free and leapt from the chair, knocking it to the floor, but she was suddenly dizzy, the dark room spinning, and just as she screamed, the speakers and woofers blasted the beat of a new chant, deep and loud and fast.

CHAPTER 4

"Karl Payne is officially missing."

Sheriff Leavitt stood six foot four, a rough beard covering his open collar, his bowling ball belly slightly larger than a moon. He let his words hang in the air for a moment then sat on the edge of Deputy Stanovich's credenza.

Four solid desks sat at even distances from each other in a large enclave at the back of the Sheriff's Office, a space that smelled vaguely of cleaning fluid and tobacco. It served as a central "war room" of sorts, a place for deputies to work on their computers, report to each other, and brainstorm problems. They'd abandoned their separate offices in favor of the new, open space, except for the dispatcher's office, where the radios were set up. Sheriff Leavitt had run the place with cool efficiency for nearly thirty years and planned to retire at the end of his term thirteen months from now. Rumors bubbled through the county about who might run for office to replace him, but no one had announced any plans.

"No sign of him in Redhorse Canyon," Deputy Dawson walked across the concrete floor, brushing dust from his pants.

Leavitt and Stanovich waited for more.

"I walked the base of the cliffs south of there, then back into the slot canyon, thinking maybe he'd gotten himself in trouble in there. Couldn't find anything but a year-old calf carcass down by the water." Dawson shuffled to his desk and laid his baseball cap on top.

"Who is this missing guy?" Stanovich asked.

Leavitt took a breath. "You left town right after high school, Stanovich, so maybe you don't remember, but Karl's been sort of a fixture in this county. A real character. Used to ranch north of here but went bust a decade ago after he lost his wife. Down and out nowadays, but always ready to lend a hand to anyone who needs it."

Grace stuck her head into the open area. "Coffee's a fresh pot, if anyone wants some." She'd been the dispatcher, front office receptionist, and all-round problem solver there for nearly twenty years.

"Grace," Leavitt's voice softened. "Have you heard?"

She glanced from Leavitt to Dawson, the question

in her eyes.

"Karl is missing."

"Oh." She clasped her hands in front of her mouth.

"We're going to find him, Grace."

Her cheeks bloomed like little pink roses. "We haven't been a thing for thirty years, Sheriff. Not since he met his wife."

Leavitt nodded. "Of course. Just thought you'd want to know, is all."

"Yes." She nodded curtly and ducked back into her office.

Stanovich squinted at Leavitt. "What am I missing?"

"Grace and Karl were engaged for a while. Many years ago, but still…"

"Oh, right." Stanovich stared at the floor for a moment, his thoughts unreadable. "So, we have a little extra reason to locate this guy."

"Sure," Dawson shrugged.

"Who reported him missing?" Stanovich's chair squeaked when he moved.

"Buck and Ron, a couple of his friends."

"Where's Karl living these days?" Leavitt asked.

Dawson scratched his forehead. "He's always been a bit of a wanderer, no permanent address as far as I know.

But he's doing some fence work for the Edwards. Stays in their bunkhouse and eats breakfast with them but they haven't seen him for three days now. Mrs. Edwards left us a detailed message."

Stanovich looked toward the sheriff. "Any chance he's just moved on to another job? Found a new place to crash?"

"Not after three days." Leavitt stood and looked at Stanovich. "Time to put a 'be on the lookout' notice for him, 'case he shows up in the next county or downtown Salt Lake somewhere. Send the BOLO to Ranger Greene in Canyonlands, too."

Utah's largest national park, Canyonlands included over 337,000 acres of mesas, spires, rivers, cliffs, canyons, and some of the strangest rock and land formations on the planet. The massive Colorado and Green Rivers carved the park into three huge districts: Island in the Sky, The Needles, and The Maze, one of the most confusing, remote, and inaccessible landscapes in America. Home to humans for 10,000 years, the area sheltered over 270 species of birds plus multiple varieties of lizards, snakes, frogs, toads, wildflowers, trees, cacti, and grasses.

Dawson lifted his hat from the desk. "I think I'll head out to Star Chart Ruins. Karl's sort of an amateur archeologist. Likes to sketch the petroglyphs. He may have gone over there for a look-see."

"No, Dawson. I want you to check out Moonshine Mesa south of there. I'll hit Star Chart."

"Sure." The Sheriff hadn't gone that far into the backcountry in ages, Dawson thought, especially by himself. He must really be worried about Karl. Or Grace.

Stanovich's eyes narrowed. "Isn't Moonshine Mesa where the explosion happened last year? Where you got shot?"

Dawson hesitated. "That's right." Stanovich had joined the Sheriff's Office shortly after the incident.

"Dawson's own version of Bigfoot was there," Sheriff Leavitt's lips rose beneath his beard, an impish grin on a grizzly bear. "In fact, the report says Bigfoot of Canyonlands National Park blew up the pumping station."

"That's not the slightest bit true," Dawson gently scolded his boss.

"So, who did blow up the station?" Stanovich spread his arms.

Dawson and Leavitt glanced at each other, a quick conversation between them.

"Dawson's the only one who's seen this desert phantom," Sheriff Leavitt said.

"Is that right?" Stanovich's chair squeaked again.

Leavitt raised a brow. "Dawson's seen him a couple

of other times, too, like in the canyon at Devil's Tail."

"Now, sheriff, I'm not the only one," Dawson raised a finger. "Archeology students, a couple of hikers, and rafters have reported seeing him, too."

Leavitt huffed. "But there are no photos of the man, just some vague descriptions. Rumor is, he runs a bunch of moonshine stills in the outback. And monkey wrenched at least one construction project in the canyons."

"So, this phantom of yours is the one creating all the mayhem I've been hearing about?" Stanovich teased.

"That's the story." The sheriff checked his sidearm. "Only next time," he nodded at Dawson, "arrest the sonofabitch, would you?"

"Can't arrest a ghost," Dawson cocked his head and turned to leave.

CHAPTER 5

"Faster," Reed barked at him, lips pulled tightly against his teeth.

"I am," Teddy panted, his legs moving as fast as he could.

The girl wasn't big, but she was out like a light, dead weight carried between the men like a drunk being led home to sleep it off.

Teddy stood just under six feet tall, his limbs thin, his back aching under the load. It took all of his energy to keep up with Reed, a six-foot-three weightlifter who sneered at Teddy's efforts.

Reed stopped so Teddy could take a breath. Each man held the girl's arm in place over their shoulders, Reed on her left, Teddy on her right.

A young man in a crew cut and a red muscle shirt walked past them, turning his head as he went, watching them.

"Girlfriend's drunk again," Reed said. "Lost her job today and now I'm the one has to deal with it."

The man nodded and turned away.

"Good thinking," Teddy whispered. He'd been trying to stay on Reed's good side but was pretty sure it wasn't working.

A man and woman crossed behind them, arm in arm, whispering to each other. They paid no attention to Teddy and Reed.

A beige minivan sat about twenty yards away, at the end of the dimly lit parking lot.

"You got her?" Reed asked, his impatient tone an accusation that Teddy wasn't strong enough to do the job.

Teddy had met Reed only two days ago, introduced by Cooper as part of the team, and he'd tried to like the man but was having little success. Reed was strong but arrogant about it and Teddy sensed an underlying violence in him that he distrusted. But this was a straightforward catch and carry, a quick ransom, nothing more. Teddy figured Reed would be fine for the job, under Cooper's supervision, but he wouldn't want to meet Reed in a dark alley, as the saying goes. Then he realized that's exactly where they were.

"Yeah, I got her," Teddy said.

Reed looked around them, his dark eyes gleaming

under a yellowed streetlamp. "Let's get this done."

"Yeah."

They resumed their march toward the van, the girl's shoes dragging sideways in the gravel.

Teddy had hung with Cooper for three or four years now, and the man wasn't brilliant, but had never steered him wrong. In fact, he'd protected him once from a police investigation; he'd said Teddy was with him on the other side of L.A. when Teddy had robbed that liquor store in Compton. He trusted Cooper, so he accepted Reed as part of the team, though something about the man unnerved him a little.

"Hey!" Another young man wobbled across the lot, skinny arms swinging as he stepped. "What're you doing there?"

They stopped and turned toward him.

"Helping our friend home," Teddy said, waving the man away.

"Sheesh okay?" His words slurred.

"Yeah, jackass, she's okay," Reed said, as they reached the side of the minivan.

The man staggered closer, his head forward, eyes squinting at the girl.

Teddy unlocked the van and opened the door.

Reed lifted her onto the floor of the vehicle and

stepped away. Teddy struggled to lay her down slowly. He tucked a fleece jacked under her head and lifted her legs inside. He turned back toward the drunk.

Reed strode toward the man with purpose.

"Hey!" the man raised his arm to protect his face and when he did, Reed punched him hard in the stomach and the man folded like a pair of kitchen tongs, butt in the air, feet and hands both flat on the ground.

Reed turned back toward Teddy.

The drunk vomited onto the gravel, moaning, coughing, and slid fully onto the dirt.

"You didn't have to do that," Teddy pointed to the drunk.

Reed smiled a wide row of teeth. "But it was fun, wasn't it?"

Teddy shook his head and hurried to close the side door. Reed started the van, and Teddy ran to the front and jumped into the passenger seat.

At least the hardest part was over, he thought.

CHAPTER 6

Hanna set her basket of cleaning supplies on the carpet and scanned the spacious living room. To her right stood a white brick fireplace, the mantle made of polished oak. Framed photographs lined the shelf and a gold, antique clock under glass rested in the middle. Above the mantle hung a coat of arms in a silver-gilded frame. In front of her, windows rose twenty feet high with a view over manicured grass and a small driving range for golfers, rows of leafy trees in the distance.

This was the kidnapped girl's home. Her parents were wealthy mineral barons who'd settled near the slopes of Beachwood Canyon. The miniature mansion had survived massive fires in Los Angeles a few years ago, an oasis among the devastation that drove so many others from their ruined homes.

The super-lucky, living so close to the un-lucky.

The family had so much money yet seemed to

work so little. The mother spent half of her time by the pool. The father hurried about but hardly spent a full workday in his home office. The girl just waltzed around with her silver spoon, wearing designer clothes, driving an expensive car, going through the motions for college like she actually needed the education to get by. Hanna, on the other hand, scrubbed, wiped, vacuumed, washed, moved furniture, and vacuumed some more, until her muscles ached by the end of each day. It didn't matter what she did, she'd never live like these people. Where was the fairness in that?

She lifted the duster and ran it across the mantle, between the silver picture frames and over the glassed-in clock, glancing at her distorted reflection. Hanna had light brown hair tied in a bun, blue eyes, and a slim physique. She'd gotten a job with Home Cleaners, Inc. only two months ago but was thoroughly sick of it. But Cooper, her on-again, off-again boyfriend, supplemented her paycheck for the other job she was doing, the one that mattered, the one that would put them in Cancun for a year with money to spare. If their plan succeeded, she thought, there finally might be a little justice in the world.

Cooper was often down-on-his-luck, an unemployed dock worker with grandiose dreams. Five years ago, his pals dressed as circus clowns and robbed six stores in Santa Monica, including one on the pier, trapping themselves there when the police arrived. What the hell were they thinking? In desperation, they dropped their clothes into the ocean and jumped in after them. By sheer luck, a fisherman rescued them before the police boat could get there. They paid the man half of their take and none of them were ever caught.

More recently, though, Cooper planned a quick kidnap of a smalltown bank manager up in Oregon and pulled it off, netting him and his crew about a hundred and fifty thousand dollars each. Sometimes he messed it up, but sometimes he worked it out, and so far, he'd never been caught. Despite his questionable choices in life, the man had a raw sex appeal too, the scent and moves of a dangerous hunter. Something about him made her weak in the knees even though her instincts told her he was bad news. She couldn't pull herself away from him. When he invited her to be part of this job, and join him in Mexico afterwards, he offered a bucket load of money and a long, steamy, romance. She'd decided to roll the dice.

She moved to a table by the white lounge chair, wiping all the surfaces she could reach, lifting lamps and statuettes to clean beneath them. She'd come back later with a step ladder for the frame on the coat of arms and the chandeliers.

Home Cleaners, Inc. catered to an elite clientele, but Hanna had passed their background checks. She'd worked about a month before she started cleaning the Manning home, which turned out to be a promising target for their plan. It was a "modest" palace with a five-car garage, outdoor pool and hot tub, guest casita, five bedrooms, two home offices, an entertainment room, and six bathrooms. Hanna shared a tiny apartment with a co-worker, a closet-sized hovel compared to the rooms she was cleaning here. When she thought about that, she could feel the resentment build. She tried to channel the frustration into perfectionism as she dusted shelves that never collected dust and vacuumed rugs that never held any mud.

Hanna and Cooper were keeping their distance from each other, for now. But the information she provided to his team—the "intel" as he called it—was absolutely vital.

Cleaners were virtually invisible to the head of the household, a tough looking little man named Brett Manning. There were times she would walk into the room, and he'd size her up like a slab of bacon then continue whatever he was doing, almost always on the phone on business. She'd heard several of those conversations, mostly about Manning's mining investments; managers, deliveries, costs, and such.

Manning's daughter was a real party girl. Hanna had volunteered to clean the young woman's room and while she did, she'd rummaged through trash and drawers and closets and under the bed, between the mattress and box spring, and behind the dressers. The girl kept her passwords on a note taped to the bottom of the middle drawer in a small desk by the window. She left her laptop on the desk. Hanna had easy access to her school and social calendar, noting times, places, and patterns in the girl's life. She'd reported all of that to Cooper.

Hanna felt like a female 007.

She'd found matchbooks from the Black Spider Lounge, a posh nightclub in West Hollywood and calendar entries on Friday nights for her to meet with friends there. Cooper said that Hanna had really made the job come together, that he was supremely proud of her. He and his pals had scoped out the popular bar. Hanna had waited outside the home last Friday and called Cooper to confirm she'd left the house and what she was wearing. They had bet she'd go to the bar, and they were right.

It was all so clandestine, so exciting.

CHAPTER 7

Malia's eyelids were caked with dried tears and muck, her head pounding like disco drums. She lay still for a moment then moved her arms sideways, back and forth across the blanket. Everything ached.

She rubbed her face with her hands and peeked through her fingers. A plywood ceiling hung above her, old varnish cracked and split like dry skin. She slid her legs off the bed and onto the floor, her stomach clenching. Slowly, she pushed herself to the edge of the cushion and sat.

Where the hell was she? Why wasn't she in the nightclub? Where was Sheila?

A narrow hallway stretched before her but ended about a dozen feet away, where a wall and a set of dark curtains blocked her view. The place smelled of dust and moldy fruit. To her left was an open door. Gingerly, she set her feet on the carpet and balanced against the wall. One tentative step forward led to another, and she could see the tiny room had a toilet and a book-sized window above it and a shower barely big enough to turn around in. What was this place? Why was she here?

Farther down the hall she came upon a kitchenette, a linoleum countertop filthy with dried food and grime. A single propane burner sat near a small sink. Next to that was an empty space the size of a hotel room refrigerator.

She was in a trailer house. A pull-behind camper that looked like it had been built in the 1990's. And last cleaned in the 2000's.

But next to the sink sat a case of bottled water that looked new. She pulled one out of the plastic wrap, twisted the top off, and put the bottle to her lips. Her first swallow drizzled down her chin and across her blouse, but the taste was divine, and she quickly guzzled the rest of it.

A folding camp chair sat in what must be the living area. Light leaked around the edges of the main window, which was freshly boarded up. A window next to the door was covered, too. A pane above the sink was open, though, one foot by one foot square, the only other light inside this dingy cardboard box.

She hurried to the open window and peered outside. Thin blue sky, a slice of heaven, and red rock cliffs to her right. Hardly the Los Angeles skyline. How drunk had she been? She remembered Sheila leaving for the dance floor and two guys coming up to the table, and then… Oh, god. They'd shot her up with something. She'd been drugged and man-handled and who knew what else? She patted her shirt and pants, reassuring herself she was still whole, still herself.

Damn.

She could see only one door that led outside. She crept toward it, listening for any sounds, any clues about where she might be.

The world was quiet.

She reached for the handle and pulled it down, up, down, to no effect, and frantically now, but still, it would not open the latch. She tried to peer through the crack but could only see the aluminum frame.

Where was her purse? Her phone?

She was blind and deaf and helpless inside this wooden crypt, locked away from her friends, her family, her home. A muscle twitched behind her neck, a tic she could not stop. A sinking feeling in her belly hardened into gravel, her arms and legs suddenly rigid as rigor mortis.

Panic flushed through her brain like firewater, and

she screamed and screamed and screamed, her voice raw and desperate until she had no more breath to expel.

CHAPTER 8

Teddy shaded his eyes and stared at the Ford "Georgetown" RV, the size and shape of a downtown bus. Red dust had caked along its undercarriage like grime on a sweaty T-shirt. The monstrosity had made the drive over washboard roads and dry creeks some thirty miles from the nearest pavement. Teddy knew that Cooper had grown up in small towns in the region and that this canyon, bordering Canyonlands National Park, was a perfect area for storing a captive—dry, remote, and private. And Cooper had contacts in two counties nearby, had backup, he'd said, for after they'd collected the ransom and abandoned the site.

The RV would be their home away from home for the next few days, their center of command. Teddy had followed behind in a black Dodge pickup truck, transportation in case they needed a fast trip for supplies or encountered mechanical problems with the RV.

A dry gully meandered several yards away. On the edge, they had placed a 1990's pull-behind trailer, perfect for their latest venture. It was a piece of junk abandoned near the highway years ago but after some new tires and minor modifications it would serve nicely as a temporary prison.

The girl was safely locked inside.

Cooper and Reed were waiting for him in the fancy RV, so he lowered his hand and hurried through the door.

"Hey, Teddy, grab one from the fridge." Cooper raised a bottle into the air. Teddy was more of a whiskey man, but when the boss offered you a beer, you took it.

"We're halfway there." Brown stubble covered Cooper's jowls, but his skull was bald as a billiard ball, like the hair on the man's head had been rendered upside down. "But I want to hear how it went down in the bar."

Reed's narrow eyes shifted from Cooper to Teddy. His thick jaw tensed and released, a nervous habit.

"Just as you said it would," Teddy began. "We got the I.D. from you by video phone and then we hung up and watched her for a while. She was with a friend. When the friend went dancing, we moved in, fast and silent like." He jabbed his hands forward, an imitation of the action. "I distracted her while Reed shot her up. She was out in a flash," he smiled. "We took her downstairs, like she was drunk, loaded her in back of the van and took her to the other parking lot, which was empty. We put her in the back cab of the truck and followed your directions."

"You stole the van, right?"

Teddy snickered. "Yep. Left it in the empty lot."

They'd rendezvoused at a gas station in Lakewood. From there, Teddy had driven the black pickup and Cooper and Reed had taken the fancy RV. They'd kept to the speed limit. No one followed them, no police tried to stop them.

Reed had come in advance of the kidnapping to scope out the canyon and prepare the site. He'd moved the 1990's camper trailer to the edge of the arroyo and blocked the wheels with rocks to keep it in place. A handy little prison, mobile if they needed it to be.

Cooper asked Teddy: "You got her all tucked away? Doors and windows nailed shut?"

"You bet," Teddy nodded. "Left her some water and toilet paper."

"You took her stuff with you, too, eh? Whatever she had at the bar?"

"Yep. She had her friend's purse, so we got both of 'em. That's all she had with her." Teddy popped the cap on his beer.

"Bring me her purse," Cooper said.

Teddy pulled a paper bag from under the sink and set it in front of Cooper. "Your girlfriend all set to go with this?"

"She's not my girlfriend," Cooper's voice dropped, "but yes."

"She's gonna keep working for the girl's parents? Even after we make the ransom call to the dad?" Teddy took a swig.

"Yep. We figure if she quits, it might look suspicious. All she has to do is play dumb, and she's damned good at that." Cooper smirked at his left-handed compliment. "I'll check in with her later on the satellite phone."

"She was sure right about her being at that bar. We were only waiting about fifteen minutes before she and her friend showed up."

"Yep." Cooper pulled a black purse from the bag and began pulling things out of it; lipstick, brushes, a small bottle, perfume, hair ties, pens. "Jeez, they get a boatload of shit in these little things." Cooper took another swallow of beer.

"Hey, boss, what about your fingerprints?" Reed asked.

"We're burning all of their stuff before we leave." Cooper pulled out a wallet with tiny flowers printed on it. He searched it and slid out the driver's license, which he handed to Teddy. He handed the cash in the wallet to Reed.

Teddy examined the license. "These pictures never do look like the real deal."

Cooper squinted, his question implicit.

"Manning's daughter. She's a lot prettier than her picture." He handed the license back to Cooper.

"And you're a lot uglier than yours," Reed chortled.

"Hey!" A voice came from outside the RV. "Anybody home?"

The men stiffened.

Reed peeked through the curtains. "It's the gaw-damned sheriff."

CHAPTER 9

Dawson slid out of his seat and stretched. Sheriff Leavitt's truck sat on level ground about thirty yards from a black and silver RV set above the dry creek bed. Dawson had parked his truck near Leavitt's.

Cliffs rose before him nearly a thousand feet, silhouetted against a morning sky. The arroyo wandered up Slickrock Canyon, curving into the high cliffs and out of sight. A bald man stood near the RV. Two other men waved. The sheriff lumbered across uneven ground, dodging sage brush and cacti, making his way toward Dawson.

"Hey, I thought I told you—you didn't need to come here." Leavitt put a hand on the corner of the truck bed and leaned on it, a little out of breath.

"Yeah, Sheriff, I know, but my shift was over last night, and I really wanted to check out these ruins. Karl's landlady said he's been coming here lately, drawing maps of the ruins and petroglyphs."

"Karl the amateur archeologist," Leavitt said.

"Yeah, Ranger Greene says he's okay, though. Respects the sites he studies and reports anything he finds to the park rangers."

"Well, I just got done talking to those guys," Leavitt nodded toward the RV. Two of the men had gone back inside. The bald man was watching them.

"What's their story?"

"Hunters."

"But—"

"They know the season's not for another month. They're out here checking it out. They're outside the Park boundary—"

"—barely."

"So, they're okay to camp for a few days."

Dawson took a breath. "Hell of an RV to drive back here."

"Yeah," Leavitt nodded.

"Well, I guess I'll go check the ruins. See if there's any sign Karl's still around here."

"I didn't see his truck," Leavitt looked from side to side. "Don't see any other vehicle out here, either, but if you want to waste your own time, go ahead," he waved a hand at Dawson.

"I'm here now. May as well double-check."

The sheriff pursed his lips. "I'm gonna tell those guys you'll be nosing around for a bit and to stay out of your way."

"I can do that," Dawson offered.

"Naw," Leavitt turned and made his way back toward the bald man, who kept his eyes on Dawson. The two men spoke for a moment.

Leavitt plodded back to his truck. "All set."

Dawson nodded.

Leavitt scratched his beard. "I'm gonna hit the road back to town and then home for the day. Anything comes up, let me know. I think I'll have Stanovich search over toward the Smith place tomorrow. And maybe at Tilton's ranch. In case Karl might have gone there for some work."

"Right. Thanks, Sheriff. See you next Tuesday."

"Oh, yeah, I almost forgot. You're off schedule for a few days. Enjoy it." Leavitt gave a quick salute, hopped in his truck, and drove away.

The bald man turned and disappeared inside the RV.

CHAPTER 10

Malia pulled herself upright, lips trembling, and stumbled to the mirror in the tiny bathroom. Waves of tears had smeared mascara down her face. On the small counter was a roll of toilet paper and a pack of wipes. At least her captors had left her something.

She blew her nose and scrubbed her face with the disposable wipes, quickly turning them black. She ran her fingers through her hair, twisting an exploded tangle into just a wild mess.

Why was this happening to her?

She took several deep breaths. She took another wipe and finished cleaning her face and neck, inspecting as she rubbed. She couldn't decide whether it was a worthy effort or a feeble attempt.

A car door slammed, muted in the distance. She moved to the small window in the kitchenette and searched outside.

Nothing.

Well, something must be out there, out of sight. A car or a truck. Were they leaving? Or arriving? And who were they?

Movement flashed across the right side of her vision. Something, someone, was out there, running low to the ground, maybe coming her way. Her muscles tensed; hands clenched. She strained to see more, but the figure had disappeared.

Who was this? Her kidnappers wouldn't sneak up to the trailer this way, would they? They'd pound on the door and issue orders. This person was in a hurry. Could it be the one who'd closed the car door earlier? Would they hurt her or help her?

She patted her pocket, checking for her phone, an instinct, a habit, a thought to call for help, but of course the kidnappers had taken it.

She spun toward the door and stared at it, willing someone to knock on the other side.

A scratch behind her, by the window.

Malia turned and jumped backwards, into the door.

A man's face suddenly peered into the trailer, eyes dark, thin goatee hanging from his chin.

They locked eyes and stared at each other.

"Who are you?" she managed to ask.

He asked: "What are you doing in there? It's all boarded up on the outside."

"I've been kidnapped! Please, please help me!"

The man's eyes clamped shut for a moment. "Shit on a shingle."

"What?" She stepped closer to the window.

"You're trapped in there?" he asked.

"Yes, yes, they've nailed the door shut. I can't find a way out of here!"

"Hang tight." His face disappeared.

She went to the window. "No, don't leave me here! Don't leave me!"

"Shhh," he stepped into view again, finger to his lips. "I'm working on it."

"Oh, oh," she whispered, bouncing on the balls of her feet. Being locked inside was terrifying but in the face of hope, the sweet anticipation of release, waiting was suddenly unbearable.

The man dropped out of view, but she could hear him scurrying around the trailer, grunting, pushing against the frame, running to the other side.

"Okay," he came back to the window. A ponytail lay on his left shoulder, the straps of a large daypack straining against his back. "I'm going to try something. Hold on. Get ready for a drop and crunch."

He moved away again.

"A what?"

The floor began to rise near the boarded window up front. She gripped the kitchen countertop and leaned forward.

Slowly, slowly, the trailer moved back one step, two steps, the front rising higher, the man grunting with effort.

"What the hell?" she forced the words through her teeth.

A third step, this time longer than the others, then another, faster now, and faster. She could feel the roll of the tires beneath her when suddenly the camp chair clattered to the floor and skidded into her knees, the window rising radically upward. She clung to the countertop as inertia tilted the trailer backwards, her feet no longer on the floor, gravity inverted as the trailer dropped into empty space.

CHAPTER 11

Dawson wandered along the row of ancient apartments, scanning the ground for signs of anything recent, any artifact of modern man. He peeked into the largest stone structure, two stories high, windows like blackened eyes of an apparition. He stepped farther back, better to see the whole pattern of homes and storage units and turkey pens.

He turned to see the fancy RV in the distance. About a quarter mile to the left of that sat a battered old camper trailer, long abandoned, no doubt. He wondered whether he had jurisdiction to have the camper removed or if it should be left to the park service but decided it had probably been there long enough that it didn't really matter anymore. He chuckled at the thought that someday the feds might protect its "historical" value. He moved back toward the ruins and followed them to the last structure in the row. Here, the cliff petered out to a blank wall of sandstone, no more natural shelter for the ancient apartments.

Hands on his hips, he stared at the site, empty of people, and sighed.

No Karl here.

He'd seen a tall granary on the southeast end of the ruins, the stonework rougher than those on the homes, a wall he hadn't noticed before. Maybe he'd just forgotten it. But he hadn't seen any sign of Karl there, either.

Maybe the sheriff was right. It was time to move on.

He turned back toward the RV when a flash of light caught his eye. Someone was inside the mobile unit, watching him with binoculars. Well, if he were in the RV, he'd be curious about what someone was doing out here, too.

Movement at the old camper trailer made him stop and squint. Did he see someone? Must be one of the hunters, checking it out.

He glanced at the ground and made his way toward a trail that ran parallel with the ruins and when he looked up again, he blinked.

The old trailer was gone.

Gone?

A faint thud echoed across the canyon.

A billow of dust rose near where the trailer had

been, but now he could see no one in the area.

A door banged shut. One of the hunters had stepped outside the large RV.

Dawson quickly began to walk toward the spot where he'd last seen the little trailer, wondering if his eyes were tired enough to play tricks on him, wondering if the hunters had seen whatever had just happened.

CHAPTER 12

Hanna moved the duster slowly over the oak bookcase, examining small statues of the Eifel Tower, the Greek Pantheon, and Japanese mini vases. She was cleaning Mr. Manning's home office, a spacious room with tall windows. A five by seven photo of a teenaged girl sat on one end of the shelves. Her features were pleasant if not a little vague, malleable. It was hard to tell for sure how she would look when she was older. The girl leaned against an outdoor fountain, water sparkling in the sunlight, gleaming with wealth. This family could afford a small fortune in ransom and not blink an eye.

She heard someone outside the door and hurried herself to the next shelf.

"Oh." Mr. Manning straightened his collar and moved behind his desk. "Didn't know you were here."

"Sorry, sir, I can finish up later." She placed her duster and a loose rag into the front pocket of her smock.

"No, no, finish up, I've got a call its but not for a bit."

"Well… if you're certain, sir. I don't want to be in the way."

He waved a hand at her, a signal for her to proceed.

She removed the duster and resumed work on the lower shelf, carefully cleaning the tops of the books, behind the little statues, and around the small picture frames. When she reached the bottom shelf, an odd feeling crept into her bones, the sense that she was being watched.

She finished as quickly as she could and stood.

"How long have you been working here?" Manning was a short, stubby man with loose jowls, a short nose, and large ears, a French Bulldog with an oxford shirt and a beet-red tie.

"Maybe a month."

She'd caught him appraising her figure once before, but this time he was blatant about it, scanning her up, down, and up again.

She felt her face redden.

"You like it here? Like working in my house?" His gaze drifted around the stately office as if to display it all.

She cleared her throat. If the man knew what she was really doing, he'd fire her in a flash. She needed to stay friendly. But not too friendly.

"Yes, it's great here." She slid the duster back into her smock.

"Where are you from?"

He was flirting with her, simple as that. A married man with a daughter, his wife in the same house with him.

"Lakewood area." She turned and pointed at the photograph on the shelf behind her, changing the subject. "This is your daughter?" she asked.

"Yes."

"She's very pretty."

"Well, she's my stepdaughter, but yes, very pretty. So are you, you know." His crooked smile exposed a canine tooth.

"Thank you." She took a step toward the door. "I'd best get to the other rooms, now."

He slid away from his desk, on a path to intercept her. "Take a break for a minute."

The office door swung open without warning, Mrs. Manning blocking the light from the hall. "There you are! We need those toilets cleaned. No more dilly-dallying." She put her hands on her hips, her eyes squinting in mild annoyance.

"Of course, ma'am." Hanna hurried past her, into

the hallway, and to the cleaning cart a few feet away.

"You have to keep on them," Mrs. Manning whispered to her husband, who grunted.

CHAPTER 13

Screeech!

The rear of the trailer struck ground, tossing her upward into the front wall. Dust exploded from every nook and joint, latches popped, cabinet doors cracked against wood, the ceiling split like a boxer's lip. Her knees scissored down hard, and her hair billowed into her face. Her feet caught the side of the countertop, now horizontal, and she balanced herself while the trailer teetered on end, creaking, moaning its own kind of pain, deciding whether to perch right there or fall the rest of the way, upside-down.

The camper swayed like a raft on whitewater.

"Hey!" The man was knocking on the wall below her, to the rear of the trailer.

The seam at the side had broken open, a cracked egg, sunlight streaming inward.

Her breaths came fast and shallow. What the hell

just happened?

"Hey! Come on!"

She slid off the side of the counter, her foot placed into the side of the bathroom doorway, feeling her way toward the cracked wall. She was stepping down a make-shift path, a staircase that should have led sideways, but it felt like Escher's Stairway, the famous drawing where steps seemed to lead downward and upward at the same time.

"This way," he yelled.

She lowered herself to the split in the wall and wig-gled through.

"Quick!"

The man grabbed her wrist and pulled her away from the trailer and up the arroyo, a black ponytail bob-bing against his collar. She waved at the dust, trying to clear it, and he pulled her farther away. They both stopped and stood there, staring at the broken thing, a beetle on its hind end, rubber legs spinning, trailer hitch pointing straight into the sky like insect antennae.

It teetered slowly at first, then in larger and larger arcs until the creature crashed flat on its back, feet in the air, guts sloughing into the dirt, red dust spilling from the inside out.

"Well, that thing's a piece of toast." The man grinned and began to trot up the dry creek bed, motioning for her to follow.

"Who are you?" she shouted, limping behind, gaining her balance as she went.

"Stop there!" A voice called from behind them.

"Don't look back," the man with the ponytail jogged faster and waved his hand, urging her to keep up.

She started running toward the guy, hoping that it wasn't a bad decision. She began to feel the fresh air, the joy of movement, running now, following the ponytail man like her life depended on it.

CHAPTER 14

Reed arrived at the arroyo first and yelled but couldn't see them anymore. Maybe they'd gone around a bend in the creek bed. Teddy and Cooper skidded to a stop behind him, the three men standing on the edge, staring at the upside-down camper trailer and a cloud of dust wafting away from them.

"What the hell?" Cooper slid his hands across the top of his cue-ball head.

"Damn." Reed pulled a Glock 19 from beneath his jacket.

"We should go after her?" Teddy asked.

"Yeah, yeah, but let me think first." Cooper turned away, his jaw clenched. "Shit. That deputy is on his way here from the ruins."

Reed squeezed the pistol grip.

Teddy turned to watch the deputy. "That cop is gonna wanna investigate."

"Yeah, that's right. So, we're gonna help him," Cooper relaxed his shoulders, shaking out his fingers. "Reed, put that away," he glanced at the gun.

Reed grunted.

"Reed, you should volunteer to help the deputy find out whatever happened here. We don't know anything, haven't seen anyone else out here. Right?"

"Right." Reed slipped the Glock back under his jacket.

"Me and Teddy will stay here. I've got a call to make on the sat phone to that girl's daddy."

"But we don't have her anymore," Teddy said.

"The deputy is going to help us with that." Cooper's lips rose. "And daddy doesn't have to know his little girl has flown the coop."

"Somebody had to help her get out of that trailer," Teddy said.

"Obviously." Cooper straightened his shirt. "We'll find him, too."

Dawson hustled toward them, across the open ground. "What happened here?"

"Just what we were trying to figure out," Cooper walked toward the deputy. "We heard the noise and came out to see."

"Woo," Dawson said as he reached the edge of

the arroyo.

They all stared at the old trailer, a dead insect on its hard, curved shell.

"Did you see who did this?" Dawson asked.

"No," Teddy glanced at his partners. "I just heard it. But somebody had to push that thing over. I mean, it was sitting close to the edge," he pointed, "but still…"

Cooper seemed to nod at Reed, a fast, subtle motion.

"I saw two people run from it," Reed said. "A man and a girl, I think. Up the dry creek bed."

"What the hell would they be doing out here?" Cooper asked.

"Just what I want to know." Dawson looked at the three men. "I'm going to follow them. We're out of cell phone range and my radio's back at my truck. Can you guys help?"

"I can take our truck back out to the highway. Maybe get a signal from there," Cooper said.

"Talk to Sheriff Leavitt. You guys met with him earlier."

"Sure." Cooper looked under his brow at Reed, a prompt for him to speak.

"I can help you, deputy, if you want." Reed shifted from one foot to the other. "I'm a pretty good tracker and if you're chasing two people, you might need a hand."

"You sure?" Dawson scanned the man, sizing him up. "It's rough country up canyon."

"I'm itching to find out what the hell is going on, too," Reed nodded.

"Okay. But you stay under my command, alright?"

"Sure."

"You okay taking orders from me, if need be?"

"Yes, sir."

Cooper reached for Teddy's arm, turning him back toward the RV. "Teddy will wait at our RV, in case they circle back. I'll get to the highway and call it in," Cooper said.

"Do you have a pistol?" Dawson asked Reed.

"Yes, sir. Just in case." He patted the gun beneath his jacket.

CHAPTER 15

"This has just turned into a giant shit show," Teddy walked behind Cooper toward their RV.

"No, no, my friend. This is one of the reasons I picked this place," Cooper glanced back. "No cell phone coverage and we're the only ones with a satellite phone."

"Now we got a deputy to deal with."

"And we have plenty of time to deal with him. Look—" Cooper stopped and checked behind them.

Dawson and Reed had already climbed into the arroyo and disappeared.

"We call the girl's daddy now with the ransom demand. Then I'll check with Hanna, who's still at their house—see how the family's reacting. I'm not going out to the road to alert the sheriff or anyone else. Daddy has six hours to transfer five million to our bitcoin account, then we're out of here."

"Now we have to wait for Reed to come back."

"True…"

"What if Reed and the cop catch her and bring her here?"

"We'll figure it out, don't worry."

Teddy stiffened. "I thought we weren't gonna be doing that."

"Doing what?"

"Hurting anybody." A shiver passed through him. "You know Reed."

"Hey, now," he drew out his words, softening them. "Nobody said anything about hurting anybody." Cooper looked him in the eye. "Shit happens sometimes. We roll with it, buddy. Don't worry. I'll take care of it." He put a hand on Teddy's shoulder. "This operation is clean as a whistle."

Teddy stared at the ground and nodded. Kidnapping a rich bitch for ransom was one thing. Beating on people was something entirely different. So long as Cooper meant what he'd said. He thought about it. Cooper could keep Reed in line. Probably. They just needed to get their payday quickly and go their separate ways.

Cooper turned and moved toward the RV. Teddy shuffled behind. They entered the RV's living quarters, and Cooper pulled two beers from the refrigerator. "Better Reed out there in all that heat and dust than us," Cooper popped one bottle and handed the other to his cohort.

Teddy took the brew.

Cooper took a long draw on the beer and grabbed a notepad with numbers on it. "Here goes." He pulled a voice modifier from his duffle bag, turned it on, and dialed the phone. After two rings, a man answered.

"Hello?"

"Mr. Manning?" Cooper's voice sounded like a robot. Teddy thought it was pretty clever, the metallic words distracting him from thoughts about what Reed might do if things turned sour.

"Who is this?"

"The man who has your daughter."

"What?"

"I will return her safely to you on one condition."

"How did you get this number? It's my private line."

Teddy leaned an ear closer to the phone. Didn't her father want to know about his daughter?

"Your daughter will not be harmed, but immediate payment is required."

"Is this a sick joke?"

The man hung up and the line disconnected.

"What?" Cooper held the phone away from his ear like it had screeched at him.

Teddy shrugged. "Maybe he doesn't know his daughter is missing, yet."

Cooper dialed again. Wrinkles formed on his bare forehead, ripples over troubled waters.

Manning shouted before Cooper could speak. "Get off this line! I'm calling the authorities."

Cooper squeezed the phone. "Not if you want to see your daughter alive."

CHAPTER 16

"Hey, wait up!" Malia ran to catch up with the man, who barely slowed.

"Who are you? What's your name?"

He turned toward her, walking sideways. "Relic."

"Like an old-fashioned phone or something?" As soon as she heard herself, she regretted saying it.

"Sure." He spun on the ball of his foot and hurried farther up the arroyo.

"Hey!" She clambered over loose rocks, panting at the effort. "What…are you…doing…out here?"

"Seems like I'm helping you."

Who is this guy, really?

"Thank you, but…can we take a break?" She wondered how this man was able to move so quickly. These rocks were brutal.

He turned again and pointed behind them. "Those guys are right on our tail."

"I'm Malia, by the way." She scrambled closer and extended her hand.

Relic gave it a quick shake. "Great. We gotta go." He tightened the straps on his pack and resumed his quick pace up the creek bed.

The bottom of the arroyo was flat but cluttered with stones and branches that were hard to avoid. Each misstep twisted her ankle or slid her toes into rocks. Her shoes were thin and flat, hardly hiking quality, her feet tired already. Walls of brown dirt and embedded pebbles rose on either side of them, about eight feet high, channeling uphill and into a curve to their left. She released a sigh and hurried to catch up.

Relic kept a grueling pace but hardly seemed out of breath. The dry creek bed eventually split into two forks. He waved her to move ahead of him, along the left side.

"Where?" she asked.

"Keep going." He moved back to the right fork and disappeared. After several moments, he walked backwards down the arroyo, a branch of sagebrush in his hand. Then he moved up the left fork and began wiping their footprints from the ground. "I said, keep going," he pointed.

"Yeah, yeah, okay." Geeze, what a bossy guy. She took a moment to search for her phone, an ingrained habit, but of course it was gone.

"Won't fool 'em for long," he jogged past her.

"Hey—" How the hell was he running uphill, with a pack on his back? She planted one foot in front of the other, sweat soaking her shirt, too winded to protest further.

CHAPTER 17

They continued up the arroyo until they reached a sharp turn to the left, where it opened to a half-circle of limestone cliff twenty-five feet high. Malia stopped to draw some air. A bowl of water the size of a child's swimming pool lay at the bottom of the small bluff, the collection point for runoff that had polished the rock above it.

"Up here," Relic pointed to a spot where shallow ridges had formed in the stone, horizontal waves in the rock.

"Really?" she asked.

"We need to get above the waterfall."

"There's no water falling here," she waved a tired hand toward the cliff.

"Right. In the spring there is." Relic lowered his hands toward her feet and cupped them together, a gesture meant to entice her with help for the climb.

She shuffled toward him. "I'm tired."

"They are not far behind us." He motioned with his hands again.

She closed her eyes and sighed. Keep going, she told herself. She moved close to Relic and placed one foot into his hands. With surprising strength, he flung her upward and held her shoe above his head. The bare rock was rough, edges sharp, but she found a narrow ledge and pulled, her free leg scrambling for purchase.

Her face pushed against a patch of damp earth, and the scent reminded her of tobacco and wet dog hair. She found a ledge with her right foot and raised herself a little higher, leaning into the bluff. Her left foot found a ledge and she reached for fresh handholds, moving a couple more feet.

"Nice work."

She grunted her reply and found another foothold. Soon, she reached the upper edge and rolled onto level ground, breathing hard.

Relic appeared moments later, standing above her. He held out his hand and she took it, rising slowly from the stone.

"You need to keep going up this drainage," he waved a hand behind him. "I'll slow them down, but I can't keep them away forever."

She looked up the canyon at a whole new landscape, the arroyo snaking its way higher into the sandstone bluffs. "Up there?" she asked, feeling stupid as soon as she said it.

"Yep. I'll catch up."

"How far? Won't they catch us sooner or later anyway?"

"No. But for now, just keep going as fast as you can."

Her voice carried a half-cup of sarcasm and defeat. "Of course."

Relic set his pack a dozen feet away from the edge of the rock shelf and began searching the ground, gathering fist-sized stones. What the hell is he doing now? He looked up at her and motioned for her to get moving, so she turned and hobbled away.

Voices floated from below the canyon, the two men chasing them. She glanced behind her and saw Relic laying stones near his pack. He'd positioned himself several feet away from the top edge of the small cliff, probably out of sight to anyone near the pool below.

She turned back to the dry creek bed and trudged farther up, where the drainage bent to the right. She stopped there before losing sight of Relic. The sounds of the men below were clearer now, some of their words echoing up the canyon.

She heard someone say, "Up there," then the sound

of boots scrambling up the cliff at the same place she and Relic had climbed.

Relic tossed a stone over the edge.

"Shit-damn!" It sounded like the man below had slipped to the bottom, dodging Relic's missile.

"Get down here!" one of the men shouted.

Relic remained silent.

It sounded like the man was climbing again.

Relic tossed another stone over the edge.

"Damn it to hell…" the man swore a mouthful of curses, each viler than the last, some of which she'd never even heard before.

The canyon grew quiet again.

Blam! A pistol shot reverberated against the sheer cliffs; her neck suddenly tense, her fingers shaking with the explosion.

She watched and listened for several moments.

"…other way…" said one of the men below.

The sound of climbing reached her again and Relic tossed another stone over the edge.

Blam! This time, the caustic blast seemed to flow right to her legs, her feet, her arms pumping, and she ran as fast as she could for as long as she could, weaving her way farther up the dry creek bed.

CHAPTER 18

Hanna squeezed the dirty water from the mop, letting it drip into the bucket below. Her nerves were on edge, but working helped to keep them in check. She'd mopped the kitchen, cleaned the counter tops, scrubbed the shower stalls in the bathrooms, and was ready for a break. But she hardly trusted herself not to reveal her secret and she needed to keep moving through the house, watching, listening.

She rolled the bucket to the slop sink and dumped the water. She closed the door and wiped her brow with a rag and stood there for a moment, collecting her thoughts.

Today was the day Cooper would make the call to Mr. Manning. She was listening for any news, any reaction from the girl's parents about the kidnapping. Cooper said he would call her with any updates from his end. Most importantly, he would let her know when the money had been transferred. She would call in sick in a few days and then give her employer proper notice to quit, so they could avoid suspicion. She and Cooper would meet in Mexico.

She took a clean cloth and spray bottle and moved into the large living area. Though she'd cleaned in here before, it was a good central spot to listen for activity, so she began dusting the table tops and lamps again, careful to take her time with the hard-to-reach spots.

Mr. Manning strode into the living room, phone to his ear, and her heart beat faster. She heard snippets of the conversation: "All right," he nodded. "Call the lawyer." He hung up and paced by the piano, shoes shushing on the carpet, spinning, shushing again, the man's eyes on the phone in his hand. The phone rang and he punched at the screen and listened.

His face turned red as an apple, eyes tight, lips pressed thin.

Hanna continued to dust, more slowly now.

"How did you get this number?"

Manning stopped for a moment then stormed toward his home office. "It's a private line!" He slammed the door behind him.

The man was not happy.

She bit her lip and continued wiping surfaces, moving across the room. She tried to stay focused on what she was doing but she couldn't help wondering whether she'd overheard Cooper's call to Manning. Five minutes later, her phone buzzed. A call from Cooper. She moved to a corner of the room and answered.

"Yeah?"

"We just made the call to Manning."

"Yeah?"

"Oddly enough, he hung up on me. I expected him to want us to prove we have his daughter."

"He's mad as a bag of wet cats," she whispered.

"Cool."

"But I just learned something." She covered the phone with her hand. "The girl is his stepdaughter."

"Ah-ha. That might explain the guy's reaction. He'll come around soon enough, though; he'll have to. We'll give him a little more time before we call again. Even a stepdaughter has to be worth something, even if it's just to keep the wife happy."

Cooper had pulled off a kidnap and ransom not too long ago. He and the crew he used at that time had whisked a banker off the dark streets on his way home from a basketball game. Cooper had told her that once sedated, the man was easy to move to an abandoned house in Boyle Heights. Cooper had dealt with the wife then, and she paid quickly. They'd left her directions to find her husband and it was all over in three days. As the saying went, Cooper could 'screw up a crowbar' sometimes, but in this instance, she figured he knew what he was doing.

She glanced around the room. "I'll be done this afternoon, but they want us back on Monday to help get ready for a party next week. Of course, they might cancel now, with the you-know-what and all, but I'll keep an ear out, for sure."

"Great going, sweetie."

She smiled at Cooper's compliment, hung up the phone, and began dusting the other side of the living room with renewed vigor.

CHAPTER 19

Dawson came to a split in the arroyo and went left about a dozen feet, then doubled back and moved up the right side. Reed had said he'd seen a man and a girl run from the trailer. There seemed to be no footprints to tell him which way the people had gone. Reed signaled to Dawson that he would follow the drainage on the left. Dawson went to the right, walking across the dry creek bed and around scattered rocks and patches of gravel. No footprints here, either. After about fifteen minutes, Dawson heard Reed shouting, returned to the split, and joined him on the left branch of the arroyo.

"They wiped their tracks part way up," Reed said.

"Bought themselves some time," Dawson nodded.

"Boot prints are clear here, though."

Dawson led the way farther up, slowing now and then to search the ground. After a while, they came upon an alcove, where the dry creek bed leveled out beneath a semi-circle of limestone cliff. In the spring, rainwater would flow in the arroyo above them, cascading over the bluff in a waterfall about twenty-five feet high. Dawson surveyed the area, searching for signs that the man and girl had been there.

Reed walked up behind him. "Any sign of them?"

"There," Dawson pointed at two sets of footprints leading to the rock wall. "They must have gone up here."

"Not much to hold onto."

"No. But they must have." Dawson stepped toward the spot where the prints ended, and the bluff began. "There isn't anywhere else…"

Blam!

Dawson leapt back and spun, his hand on his holster.

"What? Why—"

"Just letting them know we're here," Reed lowered his pistol.

Shithead, Dawson thought. He took a breath and turned back toward the cliff. "I'm going up."

"I'll wait 'till you get all the way up, then follow you."

Dawson found a foothold and began to climb the stone, fingers reaching above his shoulders for a grip. A sudden rumble sounded above him, and a rain of pebbles fell on his shoulders and across the route he'd chosen.

"Shit!" The deputy slid down the rock face and stepped quickly away from it.

Reed knelt in the sand, his Glock raised again for another shot.

"Don't—" Dawson began.

Blam!

"No shooting! You can't hit anything from down here, anyway," Dawson yelled. "The angle's too low. They're hiding up top, tossing stuff blindly."

"Bastards." Reed aimed toward the rim.

"No, now, stop!" Dawson pointed his finger at Reed, an order.

Reed's eyes moved toward the deputy, a blackened menace deep inside the man. A heartbeat passed between them. Reed lowered his gaze and his gun, nodding in agreement.

"Look for another way to the top," Dawson said.

Reed stood and they backed away, searching the slick, water-worn cliff for another route. They moved right and left, then back again, but the only possible way up was the place Dawson had tried to climb.

"They can't keep throwing rocks at us forever," Reed whispered.

Dawson nodded.

"Let me try." Reed hurried to the rock face and began to climb. In moments, more rocks tumbled down, larger ones this time, rolling past him, grazing his shoulder, just missing his head.

"Damn it." Reed slid to the ground and ran from the cliff, out of the range of the falling rocks, cursing as he went.

"Hey!" Dawson yelled. "You up there! You are under arrest! Come down now or we will haul your ass off to jail for assaulting an officer!"

They stood near the center of the alcove, staring along the rim, watching for any sign of movement. Minutes passed without so much as a scrape, a breath, a sound of any kind at all.

"Damn it all," Reed stomped his foot.

"You're right, though," Dawson turned to him. "They can't do this all day. They're going to make another run for it, higher up the canyon."

"So, we have to stand down here like a couple of jackasses?"

"For now." Dawson relaxed. "We're just gonna have to keep trying every now and then and see what happens. Sooner or later, though, we're going to get past this bluff."

"What then?"

"This is a box canyon. It ends not much farther up. Their only way out is past us and all the way back down."

Reed tucked his thumbs in his belt. "That is not gonna happen on my watch."

CHAPTER 20

Malia reached another turn in the arroyo and stopped, hands on her knees, chest heaving.

She'd heard no more gunshots, no voices, no footsteps behind her.

Blood-red sandstone rose hundreds of feet on either side of the dry creek bed, which narrowed more and more the higher she'd gone. Patches of grass clung to the earth at the base of the cliffs. Water must flood the canyon in a hard rain, she thought, swirling over boulders, scouring the bluffs, rounding the rocks. What she wouldn't give right now for a creek to dip in, a pool like the one below them to dunk her over-heated head.

Should she keep going? How far did this canyon go?

Was Relic all right? Would he be coming soon?

She walked farther along the sandy bottom, past the turn, and along another straight stretch of arroyo. When she came to a chunk of sandstone, sliced from the cliff above, she heard someone moving up the canyon. She slid behind the stone and watched.

Relic trotted up the middle of the dry bed, his pack bouncing like a rider on a horse, up, down, up, down.

She waited until he'd nearly reached her and stepped in front of him.

"Relic."

He stopped. "Good job. We gained on them back there."

"I saw you throwing rocks, but won't they come up here now that you've stopped?"

"Yep."

"So…"

"They tried to find another way up above the pool, but where we climbed was pretty much it. I waited a good while and they must have thought I'd left. Then they tried again, and I threw more over the edge again."

"They must be pretty pissed."

"Yep."

"Weren't you afraid they'd shoot you?"

"I was on top and too far from the rim for them to see me. That guy was shooting blindly at nothing at all."

"But…"

"I waited two times for them to try climbing again and rolled rocks at them each time they were part way up. I'm hoping that means they'll wait a longer time before they try again."

"But they'll keep coming?"

"That's what I figure."

"So where do we go now?" she waved her hand up the canyon.

"Just a little bit farther up."

"Not much farther, I hope."

"Follow me."

Malia trudged farther up the canyon, the walls of the dry creek bed lowering and narrowing as she went. Her blouse dangled loosely from her shoulders except under her arms, where it kept sticking to her skin. She hadn't felt this sweaty or dusty since she was nine years old, playing on the softball field under an August sun.

Relic was out of sight, beyond another curve, but his footprints were clear and there was nowhere else to go but up. Her path angled to the left for a bit, and something made her stop.

The dry bed petered out at the edge of several long sandstone slabs, sliced from a ring of cliffs like chunks of cheese chiseled from a thousand-foot-high block. A patch of grass, long and green, rose along the wall to her right, a spot where water must seep through the rock formation, but the rest of the ground was dry. Cacti and cheat grass were scattered across the dirt like they'd been tossed by an impatient gardener. The gorge was cut into a tight semi-circle, maybe thirty yards across. Sheer, red walls reached to the sky. Her head became dizzy from staring upward.

The man had taken them into a dead end. What kind of simpleton was she following?

"This way." His words startled her.

He'd removed his pack and was tying a rope to it.

She forced her legs to step forward, stiff and tired, feet plodding against the hard dirt.

"I'll go up first—"

"—first?"

"—and pull my pack up, then I'll lower the rope to you. You'll need to wrap it under your armpits and tie it tight."

"What?"

"Once we get past that slick spot," he pointed at the canyon wall, about a hundred feet above them, "there's a nice ledge that takes us to a sheep trail and on to the top."

She arched her neck back, eyes toward the bare rock wall. "You're joking."

"Those guys will be here soon. We've just enough time, if we hurry."

Relic tied the other end of the rope to his belt and

began to climb the cliff, jamming his boots into fissures, reaching for handholds she could barely see.

She plopped to the ground and released a long, tired breath.

Pebbles clattered to the rocks below as Relic made his way upward and toward an outcrop that had detached from the cliff. The man climbed with the agility of an ant, and then he disappeared.

Slowly, the rope became taut. Relic reappeared on a ledge, tugging the pack. It snagged on a rock part way up and he whipped the rope once, twice, until it dislodged. Eventually, the pack reached his hands, and he set it aside. He untied the line and threw it back down to her.

She stared at the toy-sized figure above her on the sheer cliffs, rope dangling between his legs.

There was no way in hell she was going up there with that guy.

CHAPTER 21

Stanovich pulled his Sheriff Office Jeep to a stop, brown dust rising in the air. The DeMille Ranch was a two-thousand acre spread backed up against federal land managed by the BLM. The place had been established in 1886, the original home now a bundle of logs overgrown with weeds. The current house was a modest clapboard with a shiny roof, copper-colored metal sitting like a brand-new hat on an old man's head.

He got out of the Jeep and dusted off his pants.

Sheriff Leavitt had told him to come here to search for Karl, the missing ranch hand and former boyfriend of Grace, the office dispatcher. Stanovich wondered whether anyone else would get this much attention from a simple report that a wandering handyman could not be found at his home.

Mrs. DeMille was a widow with three sons who'd helped her with the ranch until a couple of years ago, when, according to Leavitt, two of them moved to Salt Lake City and one to San Diego. They'd tried to get her to a retirement home in Salt Lake, with no luck. Leavitt said she was stubborn as a mule. Stanovich remembered the youngest, Barry, who'd been a year older than Stanovich in grade school.

Mrs. DeMille came to the door, opened it, and waited. She wore faded jeans, boots, and a worn plaid shirt. Her white hair was tied in a tight bun at the back of her head, her cheeks as wrinkled as a road map.

Stanovich waved and walked toward her with a smile. He'd called ahead to make sure she was home and had time to talk with him today.

"Stan?" she asked, hand on her chest. "Oh, my god, that is you. I remember you as a little tyke."

Stanovich tipped his hat. "Yes, ma'am. Barry brought me out here once or twice to ride, when we were kids. That was a helluva long time ago."

She smiled a row of coffee-colored teeth. "Don't tell me how long ago! Look at you now," she pointed to his uniform. "All official and formal!"

"Yes, ma'am."

A dog with pointed ears peeked from behind the woman, its tail wagging. He knelt and it came to him, some sort of German Shepard mix. He scratched its head and stood again.

"Come in for some tea!" She went back into the house and held the door open.

He went inside, the dog following his every step.

"Come sit for a minute and tell me how you've been."

Stanovich moved to the small living room. A wood-stove anchored the far wall. Two stuffed chairs sat nearby, facing each other, white doilies draped across their backs. Photos of her boys hung near the doorway, high school portraits, he guessed. He took the chair closest to him and the dog plopped onto the carpet, no longer fascinated with the latest visitor.

Mrs. DeMille brought iced tea and a box of Girl Scout cookies and grilled him for fifteen minutes: When did he come back home? Was he married? How did he like working for Sheriff Leavitt? What was it like, fighting crime in the countryside? The woman could have been a police interrogator—the "good cop" in the equation—but his answers didn't seem to stay with her for long. Soon enough, she was asking the same things over again, surprised by his answers as if they were new.

"Listen, Mrs. DeMille, it's great to catch up with you, but I'm here looking for Karl Payne. I understand he does some work around the ranch for you?"

"Of course. But what do you want with Karl?"

"Two of his friends have reported him missing. They're worried about him."

"Oh, dear, he's not missing." She flapped her hand at him, dismissing his concern.

"No?"

"No, no. I saw him yesterday. He's helping me with repairs on the corral, out back."

"Yesterday, you say?"

"Well, yes." She put a finger to her lips, considering the question. "What day is today?"

"Friday."

"No, no, it must be Tuesday. My ladies' group was yesterday, and we meet on Mondays."

Stanovich waited.

"Today…oh! They'll be here any minute. This week, we meet at my house."

"Monday?"

"Yes."

"The ladies should be here by now."

"Mrs. DeMille, today is Friday."

"That can't be." Confusion clouded her eyes. "I saw Karl yesterday."

"Last Sunday?" he asked.

"No, no," her hands clasped in her lap. "Now I'm

not sure."

"Today is Friday."

"Oh. Friday." Her lips clamped tightly together. "All right then."

"So, you saw him yesterday? Or last Sunday?"

She beamed a wide smile. "I have no idea anymore, Sheriff. Would you like another cookie?"

CHAPTER 22

Malia stood slowly, her legs shaky, and brushed the sand from her pants. Did she really have to scale this cliff? Couldn't she hide among the rocks down here? But for how long? What if her kidnappers came here and searched? Could she stay hidden and wait them out? What had she ever done to deserve all this?

Voices echoed from lower in the arroyo, startling her. She couldn't hear the words, but they were urgent.

Shit.

She approached the rope and wrapped it under her arms and tied the only kind of knot she knew. When she looked toward Relic, he took up the slack and motioned with his hands, urging her to climb.

A level rock lay near her feet, so she moved to it and stepped on, reaching, searching for a hand hold. Her fingers found purchase above her. She lifted her foot to a ledge on her right and pulled upward until she could straighten her knees. She was grateful that she'd opted for leggings the other night or she might not have been able to move this way at all.

She noticed cracks and rough edges in the cliff she'd not seen from a distance. Relic was keeping the rope snug, lending her a modest sense of security. She tried to follow where Relic had climbed but she hadn't paid close enough attention to the route he'd used.

Her fingers searched the bluff again until she found a thumb-wide ledge and lifted herself a little higher. Her whole world compressed to a few inches before her face, grains of sand, red, black, tan, compacted into a solid mosaic. She worked her way a little higher, then a little more, using her legs as much as she could, sweating through her blouse again. She wished she had gloves to protect her skin from the ragged surface that was rubbing her palms raw.

After several minutes, she'd lost all sense of where she was on the cliff or how much farther she had to go.

She twisted away from the sandstone and glanced down. The jumble of rocks below seemed to spin in a circle, gravity tugging her sideways. She quickly closed her eyes and pressed her cheek back against the cool slab.

Don't do that again.

Take a breath.

She found a shelf near her right foot and stepped on it, rising a few more inches.

Voices rose from the canyon, sharper this time.

"Keep going. You're doing just fine," Relic said.

She leaned her head back, searching the rock above, but couldn't see him. Pressing against the wall, she found another handhold and pulled.

"Try again."

She pulled once more and this time, the rope slid taut against her chest and Relic lifted her as she climbed, easing the effort. The knot was close to her face now.

A narrow rim appeared just below her knee, so she lifted her foot onto it and stood when suddenly she slipped, shoulders banging against the rough stone, hands scrabbling for a hold, hanging by the rope alone, panic coursing through her. The line dug into her armpits and back, stinging hard. Her right foot found a two-inch wide shelf and she straightened, locking her knee in place.

She wanted to surrender, right then and there on the barren rock. The whole farce was impossible; no way to escape the kidnappers, no way to keep moving when her muscles were ready to shut down. She could fall to her death and final relief.

"Almost there." Relic's voice was closer, now.

She found another ounce of energy and lifted herself on another hand hold, the line still taut against her weight, Relic helping.

But the rope was sliding slowly through her makeshift knot, closer and closer to the end. Blood rushed through her cheeks, and she grabbed the line above where it was tied, but try as she might, she could not keep it from slipping.

"Hurry."

Her feet clawed against the canyon wall, searching for a grip, her right hand reaching above her.

She rose a little higher.

The rope was nearly through the bunched knot, sliding at a steady rate.

Another tug from Relic lifted her and she found purchase with both hands and with his help, did a chin-up on the rock slab where he stood. Her foot found another hold and she rose again as the rope wiggled closer and closer to the knot, sinking into it, reaching its end.

"Here!"

Relic reached for her hand as the tangle fell loose and suddenly disappeared, unraveling, the rope whipping around her as the end fell limply to the side of the bluff.

He grunted hard, boots scrambling in the dirt, tugging her forward, and she shoved herself up to the edge of level ground and onto her stomach. Relic pulled her farther until her feet no longer dangled over the cliff, and she collapsed in the dust, panting like a racehorse.

CHAPTER 23

Deputy Dawson rested his hands on his hips and searched the cliffs above them. Reed walked toward a small seep, green with fern-like plants and velvety moss. They'd reached the end of the drainage, stopped in an alcove rimmed in a three-quarter circle by sandstone walls.

"Where the hell are they?" Reed scratched his head.

"Footprints end over there," Dawson pointed.

"They turn into mountain goats all of a sudden?"

"Looks that way."

"Damn."

"Yeah." Dawson listened for signs of movement anywhere in the canyon, but the air was silent as death itself. The afternoon sun washed the walls in auburn hues. Shadows darkened the western rim in a ghostly half-light. This disappearance was strange. Nobody could get out of the canyon here; it seemed impossible. He wrinkled his face, trying again to see any movement above the sheer walls. He wondered if the strange man with the ponytail that he'd been chasing all these years could be one of the people they were following now. That was the only man he'd ever seen who could disappear in a box canyon this way.

Dawson shook his head.

"Now what?" Reed stepped into the shadows.

"We head back down to the fork in the drainage." Dawson turned toward him. "And take the other way to the top."

"What other way?"

"The right fork continues straight for a bit then eases its way up. They must have had a rope to get up this cliff but it's only going to take them to the same place we'll get to by going back and taking the right side of the arroyo."

Reed screwed up his nose. "So, why didn't they just take the right side of the wash? They were ahead of us, after all."

"Fair question. Maybe they needed to get someplace to hide. Or to rest." Dawson thought about that.

They stood quietly for a moment.

Dawson looked at Reed. "And you're sure you haven't seen either of them before now?"

Reed hesitated. "No."

Dawson nodded.

"Now we have to back-track?"

Dawson knelt to the ground and lifted a pebble, squeezing it between his fingers. "It's the only way to get to the top, at least from this area."

Reed watched him, eyes under his brow.

"The sun's gett'n low." Dawson stood and tossed the pebble aside. "Let's get going."

Dawson led them out of the small chapel of rock and down the dry creek bed they'd just climbed. They reached the bluff at the little waterfall and helped each other down to the pool below. After another hour, they came upon the split in the arroyo. They each found a rock to sit on.

"We're gonna have to decide what we want to do," Dawson began. "Camp rough tonight, start in the morning, or try to get back to your trailer."

"It'll be dark before we get there," Reed said.

"True enough. But there might be enough light to follow this old creek bed. We could see the trailer if your friends are there with the lights on."

"Tricky ground."

"Yeah, and twisted ankles are a factor. But your pal should have talked to the sheriff by now. Maybe they get here by morning, and we start a proper search – call for reinforcements and get a drone in the air or get some help from one of our local pilots."

Reed was quiet for a while.

The distant sound of boots on gravel carried on the still air, coming up the arroyo. Both men put their fingers on their pistols and watched to see who would come around the corner.

CHAPTER 24

Deputy Stanovich moved a tangle of paperclips and a stack of reports on Grace's desk, clearing a space, and set a box of donuts there. Grace entered through the front door, brushing short, gray hair away from her face.

Stanovich hooked his thumbs in his belt. "You're here early," he said.

"You are too." She walked behind her desk and looked at him. "Damn Chevy has left me stranded again. Had to catch a ride with Doris, which puts me here thirty minutes early."

"What's wrong with your car?" he asked.

She grimaced. "You should ask what's right with it. The list is shorter."

"So, get a new one." He leaned against the wall near the radio equipment.

She glanced around the office, making sure they were alone. "So, tell the Sheriff to get us a decent raise."

"Oh," Stanovich raised the palms of his hands, "I am with you there, Grace. I don't know how long I can keep working for this outfit. You doing any moonlighting?" he asked.

"Not yet. But it's not a living wage, anymore!" She settled into her chair. "It's gotten to be, I can hardly afford to work here. I ought a to be out robbing banks or something."

He shook his head. "I know, I know. But, in the meantime," he pointed at the box, "I did get donuts."

"You're a hidden gem," she reached for an eclair. "Be a dear and turn on the coffee pot, would you?"

He gave her a silent salute, clicked on the coffee, and walked to the main room, where he shuffled across the floor to his desk. He plopped into the old leather chair and leaned back, pondering Grace's decrepit Chevy and his own broken-down pick-up truck.

The bang of a door pulled Stanovich from his thoughts. Sheriff Leavitt entered the open office space and began removing his coat.

"Any news?" Stanovich asked.

The sheriff tossed his jacket onto a chair and made his way to the coffee maker. "Nada. Nothing."

"You went to the Star Chart Ruins?"

"The canyon, yeah." He poured a cup from

the carafe.

"Nobody there?" Stanovich took an empty mug from his desk and joined the sheriff.

"No, there's a group of three hunters out there. Surprised to find them."

"Oh?" Stanovich emptied the last of the pot into his mug.

"Yeah, but they're okay, I think."

Stanovich cleared his throat.

"They're camping just outside the park boundary. Scoping it out for hunting season."

"Oh, good."

"Well, I don't know why they brought a fancy RV all the way back there, but it made it in one piece. Lucky they hadn't broken an axle."

Stanovich put the mug to his lips and blew on it.

"They hadn't seen anything odd, let alone Karl, our missing man, so…" he shrugged. "How about you? Any luck with Mrs. DeMille?"

"Not really. Nice enough lady but not sure which day of the week it is. Said she'd had him doing some work for her recently but couldn't remember when."

"Huh. A bust."

"Yep."

"Well, we've got other cases to deal with, too. I

need you to check out a broken window and theft of liquor, over at the T-Bone Bar. Walt Booker's the owner, so start with him, then see if there might be any witnesses. Walt will need a report for his insurance claim, too."

"Will do."

"Tomorrow, get back on the missing person case. I'll have you check with someone else that Karl does odd jobs for."

"Sure. And what about Dawson? Did he find anything?"

The Sheriff narrowed his eyes. "How did you know about Dawson?"

"What?" Stanovich held the coffee mug with both hands, keeping them steady.

"Dawson came out to the canyon as I was leaving. How did you know?"

"I didn't, sir," Stanovich's words were a little louder than he meant. "I just wondered what Dawson found at Moonshine Mesa."

"Oh," Leavitt turned toward the countertop and added powdered cream to his coffee. "Right. He didn't find anything there, but then he decided to stop at the ruins on his way home."

"I see, sir."

"As I'm sure you noticed, Stanovich, Dawson can

be an odd duck sometimes. I teased him again the other day about searching for Bigfoot. He claims there's a moonshiner hiding in those canyons and likes to chase that ghost."

Stanovich took a sip of coffee, watching his boss.

"I'm just saying," Leavitt added.

"Right."

"Dawson's a good egg, though. You two should hit it off pretty good."

"I'm looking forward to working more often with him."

"Good." Sheriff Leavitt turned to leave.

"But what's he doing out at the ruins? Just looking for that guy who's missing?"

"Yep. But he's off the work schedule, as you know, so he should be home by now for his weekend off." Leavitt nodded on his way out the door.

"Why would Dawson check an area that you've already checked?"

"He's a little odd, Stanovich, I told you that." The door closed hard behind him.

"Is that all it is?" Stanovich asked the empty room. "Or did he see something up there that was out of place?"

CHAPTER 25

Relic pulled the rope back up the cliff, rolled and tied it neatly, and clipped it to his pack. They set off along a ledge that widened as they went and walked for what felt like an hour, up, down, around loose boulders. Malia placed one foot before the other, certain her shoes had turned to concrete blocks. Relic waved her forward, but she wasn't sure where they were going or why they were going there or whether she could carry her body any farther.

"We're here." He stepped around the corner of a large rock and disappeared.

"Thank god," she said, and then realized she was going to have to drag herself at least a dozen more steps. She leaned against the large stone, pushing herself around it.

"Here," Relic waved toward a flat area at the base of a low cliff. Across the way, strange rock formations rose in the evening sky like claws, banded in gray and rose-colored stripes. She shuffled near the base of the cliff and dropped to the ground.

Relic slid his pack onto the sand beside her and pulled out a bottle of water. "Don't drink too fast."

She twisted off the lid and poured it down her throat until she had to take a breath. Warm, with a faint taste of salt or other minerals. Or sweaty socks.

Relic tossed a few sticks near her feet and wandered off; she assumed in search of more wood. She scooted to the bluff, leaned her back against it, and pulled her knees to her chest. She'd been sweating and now she was cooling fast.

Her hand went to her pocket, a trained reaction, a search for her phone that she knew was not there. No calls for help, no music, no video clips, no slot machine play.

Relic returned and dropped some thick branches on the ground. He began lifting book-sized rocks and stacking them in a circle. When he seemed satisfied, he laid branches into the fire ring, placing them like a miniature log cabin. He filled the center with grass and twigs then jogged away.

What the hell is she doing way out here? Why can't she just go home?

A heavy sun slid deeper into the horizon, projecting its fiery glow on the tall stone barbs, a giant hand reaching for the sky. The callous surface beamed with shades of scarlet and lemon, a complexion she'd never seen before.

Shadows slowly expanded and slipped around lumps in the sandstone until the colors began to dull, the blaze now cast upward against a row of cotton clouds.

What is this strange place?

The sun finally disappeared, the clouds a soft shade of pewter against the cooling sky.

Relic returned again, this time with an armload of dead cedar and sagebrush. He laid it near the cliff and moved to the firepit. He lit the center, blowing gently to expand the flames. The little fire flickered into a warm blaze, darkening the outer world but lighting the ground around them. Fluttering shadows exaggerated his nose and deepened his eye sockets. His expression seemed to shimmer with unknowable emotions.

Who is this guy? Is he dangerous? First, she was at the mercy of those kidnappers. Now, she was completely dependent on this character, this cave man of the desert. The stringy goatee made her think of sasquatch. Worry filled her mind with awful possibilities.

"You're not going to hurt me, are you?" she whispered.

He stared at her for a moment. "Are you kidding?"

She shifted her butt in the dirt. Was her question stupid?

"I just got you out of that prison-on-wheels." He lowered his brow. "You're not some kind of 'professional victim' are you? Expecting everyone you meet to try to hurt you?" he asked.

She recoiled. "Of course not. What are you, some kind of psych…" she stuttered, "psychologist?"

He turned and poked the fire with a stick, speaking softly: "I'm just a student of human nature."

"Way the hell out here?" She spread her arms. "I don't see a lot of humans to study out here."

"Exactly," he chortled. "I've done my homework."

"Oh." She stared at her battered shoes for a moment, then understood. The man was avoiding human nature altogether. Her cheeks flushed and she released a quick chuckle.

"Well, now I have to let you live." Relic's teeth gleamed in the ambient light.

"What?"

He shook his head with mock regret. "I never could hurt a human with a sense of humor."

They sat in silence for a beat, then she coughed, laughed, and touched her aching ribs.

"Hungry?" he asked.

"Yes." His playful mood surprised her, and the offer of food reaffirmed him as a friend, or at least an ally. She wasn't sure she had the energy to eat, but she had the willpower to try.

He handed her a stick of jerky and she chewed on the rough meat with unrestrained lust. He pulled a small pot from his pack and added water and something else to it. He placed it near the fire to cook.

"Who are you, again?"

"People call me Relic." He stroked his thin goatee.

"Interesting name. Are you really old?"

"Maybe. Like most things, it depends on your point of view."

"How did you find me? In the old trailer, I mean."

"I was hikin' near Star Chart Ruins when I saw three men in a fancy motor-camper-type thing. Shiny and new. I noticed the old trailer on the edge of the arroyo, about a quarter of a mile away. It was moving," he lifted and lowered his hands, "up and down, and when I checked it, I saw you inside, shouting for help."

"Yeah," she mumbled. "I could hear you moving stones or something and then you pushed me over the edge. I guess you were hoping the old trailer would crack open."

He nodded.

She swallowed. "I didn't understand what you were doing at first."

"When the trailer went into the arroyo, the side split apart, and you came out. Like a baby bird comes out of its egg."

"Hmmph."

"And that's when I heard those guys coming and we ran."

"Thank you."

"What happened?"

"I've been kidnapped. Was kidnapped, I mean."

"No shit." His dark eyes widened. "Why?"

"I don't know. I assume for money."

Relic took a spoon from his pack and stirred the pot.

"I guess you don't know those guys."

"No, of course not. Two men came over to my table at a bar, a place my friend and I were at, and one of them shoved a needle in my arm."

"Shit on a shingle."

"After that, I don't remember anything except waking up in that trailer. And screaming my head off."

He pulled a tin bowl from his pack, blew out the dust, and spooned whatever was in the steaming pot into the bowl. He handed the food and spoon to her and shrugged.

She stared at the bowl, dented and scratched like a cat's toy. There was no way she was going to eat that stuff.

"Nothin' fancy," he said.

Her stomach grumbled, overruling all votes against the meal. She blew on the mush-like substance and took a bite. Instant potatoes with a hint of cheddar. And a few gray specks of ash for extra flavor.

CHAPTER 26

"It's Cooper," Reed announced. They'd heard his boots clomping up the arroyo to the place they were resting, where the drainage split into two branches.

Cooper stopped to catch his breath and waved. Dawson and Reed walked toward him.

"Any luck?" Cooper asked.

"No! Slippery buggers climbed up a cliff and got away from us," Reed said.

Cooper's eyes grew large.

Dawson hooked his fingers on his belt. "They must have had a rope. We couldn't follow them, so we came back here. But this arroyo leads to the top if you follow the right side of the drainage. We can get to them, but not before we lose the sunlight."

"Maybe this will help." Cooper slipped a heavy pack off his back. "Got food, water, a light tarp and sleeping bag, flashlight, some first aid. Deputy, the pack from your truck is tied onto the outside, in case there's something in there you need."

"Wow, yes, thanks. Did you get in touch with the sheriff?"

"No, but I sent Teddy to do it."

"Is he in contact with the sheriff?"

"By now, I'm sure of it. He took the pickup toward the highway to get a signal. I didn't waste any time waiting on him but came straight here. That was okay, deputy, wasn't it?"

"Yes, perfect, actually."

"Good." Cooper nodded at Reed. "You guys must be tired out."

"So, here's the plan," Dawson looked up the arroyo. "I'll find a good camp for the night. You guys can stay or go as you like. I'll pick up the trail in the morning."

Cooper took Reed's arm and led him away from the deputy. "Let's chat about who wants to keep searching."

Dawson lifted the pack and trudged up the side of the drainage to a flat area a few feet above it and out of earshot.

"What's happening?" Reed whispered.

"Teddy did not go up the road to try to call the sheriff," Cooper looked up at Dawson, who was emptying the pack on the ground, sorting through it.

"I figured that much."

"Right. Here's the thing. The girl may or may not have had a good look at you and Teddy when you nabbed her, but the deputy up there sure as hell has had plenty of looks at the three of us since he showed up."

Reed's lips twitched.

"We left the ransom demand, though the father's reaction was a little weird."

"Weird?"

"He heard the demand then we lost the call. It sounded like he might have hung up."

"That would be odd. But the signal in these canyons…"

"I called again and made it all clear to the guy, then we lost him again."

"Huh."

"Yeah, that's probably the issue—bad signal even with the sat phone. Anyway, I'll make another demand tomorrow. We'll find a way to monetize that woman."

Reed's chest heaved a chuckle. "Monetize," he repeated.

Cooper spoke without moving his lips: "So, the deputy can I.D. us."

Reed glanced about. "The plan?"

"You stay with the deputy and together maybe you

find the girl and whoever helped her escape. But there's no way any of them can survive the trip. Right?"

"Right."

"Once it's done, get your butt back to the trailer, and we'll all get the hell out of here. And get the deputy's keys to his truck. We may want to hide it, drive it off a cliff or something."

"What if we can't find the girl?"

Cooper thought for a moment. "Maybe the deputy dies, and they figure that whoever helped the girl escape killed him. The deputy has been chasing them, after all."

"And the deputy's the only one who can I.D. us for sure," Reed said.

"Exactly."

"How long do we try to find the girl?"

"Tomorrow's Saturday. Give it until sometime Sunday, then go to plan B. We can get out of here by Tuesday at the latest."

Reed's mouth rose in a murderous smile.

CHAPTER 27

Malia reached for her phone, another ghost sensation pressing against her fingers.

"What are you looking for?" Relic placed another branch on the fire.

"My phone. I'm so used to it being here, I keep reaching for it."

"You have someone to call?"

"I can't call *anybody* way out here." *Smart aleck.* "But I have games downloaded onto it, and pictures."

Relic stroked his goatee. "You know why people love their little phones?"

"I have a feeling you're going to tell me."

"Because they are little. Because our minds can conceive of them, regulate them, be occupied by them."

"Oh? Are you going to tell me they're evil or something? The newest addiction?"

"No, not evil. They're just our latest thing. As a

species, we don't like to dwell too much on what we can't control or what we can't hold in our minds, so we focus on our own creations. They capture our attention and keep us busy in comfort."

"That's bad?"

"No, it's human. It's understandable. We all do it, we need to. But if we *only* focus on the stuff we can comprehend and manipulate, we lose our sense of wonder. Our place in this immense universe."

"First, I accused you of being a psychologist. Now I think you're a philosopher."

"Not even close. Like I said, I'm just an amateur. A student of human nature. We like our gadgets a little too much sometimes."

"But the phone has A.I. built into it. A.I. pushes the old limitations."

"A.I.?"

How long has Sasquatch been in this back country? "Artificial Intelligence."

"Oh, yeah, I *have* heard of it." Relic was quiet for a moment. "But artificial intelligence doesn't stand a chance against natural stupidity."

She laughed. "It helped rebuild a famous cathedral in Europe last year."

"You want to see a real cathedral?" he asked.

"Out here?"

"Where else?"

"Sure."

Relic stood and motioned for her to follow. She rolled onto all fours, gathering her tired legs beneath her. Where the hell were they going now?

He led her across the plateau, maybe forty yards from their little fire. Although it was a moonless night, a subtle glow had spread across the open ground. She was surprised she could see without a flashlight.

"This is a good spot." He lay onto the ground and crossed his hands on his chest.

Gingerly, she lowered herself and her aching joints to the sand and lay back.

"Close your eyes and clear your mind for a minute. Leave your thoughts back at the fire. Then, when you're calm and open-minded, look above us."

She did as he asked, taking slow breaths, counting to twenty, dropping her tired thoughts like weights.

She opened her eyes, and the sky burst forth with thousands upon thousands of stars, all sputtering flames among the purest black of space she'd ever seen. Stars on her left, her right, at her feet, beyond her head, an inverted bowl of the cosmos suspended above them. Instinctively, she reached her hands into the air as if to touch them, but the blackness had moved beyond her power of sight, countless, spinning suns beyond her power of imagination.

Relic shifted. "There are more stars in the midnight sky than all the grains of sand in all the beaches in all of the shores of all of the lands on earth."

The longer she stared, the more lights appeared, dimmer than the rest, but just as real. A swath of luminescence, the spooky glow of four hundred billion suns, was smeared above the horizon to their right.

The Milky Way.

She felt like the earth gave way beneath her, dropping into the unknown, her essence untethered from the familiar, the human network, the social web of comfort and complacency. She had no words, no labels, no descriptions for what she was seeing and feeling.

"I can't count them all," she croaked.

"We can't *conceive* of them all. The universe is beyond the capacity of the human mind."

"This is your cathedral?"

"This is the cathedral of creation. Man's imitations only prove our limitations."

Four shadows blanked out part of the sky, the sandstone hoodoos, the fingers she'd seen when they first arrived at camp. Funny how the absence of starlight let her "see" the weird formations. An orange flame pulsed on the ground beneath them, her and Relic's tiny, tiny campfire in a tiny, tiny alcove on a spinning, miniature planet.

She'd seen the dark of night in Los Angeles, of course, but never more than two or three stars at a time. And never more than a few feet from the lights of a house, a car, a streetlamp. This was entirely different. This was entirely new.

She had absolutely no idea.

How could anything built by man compare with the midnight sky?

She had to remind herself to breathe.

CHAPTER 28

Weary of the game of solitaire, the only one available without cell service, Teddy closed his phone and set it on the table. Dusk had advanced into darkness, so he turned on the lights over the front door of the large RV and over the kitchen stove. He opened the door and peered into the shadows outside, searching for a roving flashlight or any other sign of activity.

Cliffs above the ruins had blackened with the setting sun, the upper rim but a faint contrast against the peach-tinted sky. The arroyo that led deep into the canyon had become a wall of unknowable shadow.

Where the hell was Cooper? Had he decided to spend the night camping out with Reed and the Deputy?

Teddy went back inside and pulled a can of stew from the cupboard. He poured the contents into a pan and lit the propane stove. He pulled a flask of whiskey from the cabinet and stirred the thick soup with a spoon.

When it steamed, he scooped it into a bowl and sat on the narrow couch in the living area and took his time eating the soup and sipping the liquor.

He finished his stew and put the bowl on the kitchen table.

He shook his head. Who could have helped the girl escape? Whoever had done it didn't have a bolt cutter. Teddy would have used a bolt cutter, for sure. That way, the escape would have been quiet. And simple. But the man had pushed the old trailer off the edge of the arroyo, splitting the side open like a dropped melon. Alerting them to the escape. Was the man a hunter? A hiker?

He swallowed the last of his whiskey and poured another.

He hadn't met Reed before this job, but he could tell the man had a streak of mean in him a mile wide. He had no doubt the guy could kill the girl if he caught up with her. And whoever helped her escape. Why was Reed chasing them? At first, maybe he'd just been pressured into helping the deputy. But the more Teddy thought about it…

Teddy had signed on for the snatch and grab and a big payoff, but that seemed to have evaporated before his eyes. He wanted nothing to do with killing. Cooper had promised him there would be no real harm to anyone, including the girl. But would Reed keep that bargain?

Boots dragged across the dirt outside the trailer and Teddy jumped to his feet. The door opened and Cooper stepped in, shoulders slumped, eyes bloodshot and tired. He tossed his flashlight onto the couch and grumbled.

"Boss! I looked for you outside."

"I found a little trail by the ruins and came around that way."

"Come in, let me get you a beer."

Cooper plopped onto the couch and stretched his legs in front of him.

"Here," Teddy handed him the bottle and stepped back, waiting for news.

"Damned hiking. Whoever invented that?" Cooper took a swig. "Ahhh."

"Are you okay? What happened? Did Reed stay with that officer?"

Cooper raised his hand, a signal for Teddy to wait, and took another long drink. "Yeah, I'm okay, I guess. Didn't know I was that out of shape."

"And Reed?"

"He's camping with the deputy. They're going to search again in the morning for the girl and whoever helped her."

Teddy nodded. "I've been thinking about that."

"Yeah?" Cooper took another swallow.

"What happens if they find them?"

"Teddy, look. Reed will find a solution, all right? Then he'll come back, and we'll get the hell out of here."

He thought about that phrase: "find a solution." Teddy knew just what that meant. Cooper was going back on his promise. Teddy was going to be some kind of accessory to murder.

He turned away so his boss couldn't see his face.

CHAPTER 29

SATURDAY

Relic had given her a fleece jacket and one of those thin "space" blankets to wrap around her. She'd turned her back to the fire, rested her head on her arm, and fallen into a deep sleep.

A dream as vivid and real as waking life slipped away from her, forever lost in the folds of memory. Soft light, beyond her eyelids, brought her into another dream, it seemed. Cautiously, she opened one eye and tried to focus.

Sandstone filled her view as she remembered the day before. Relic. Their run up the canyon. Her climb up the cliff. The rope that helped her reach the top. Then, a blazing sunset, warm fire, and food.

She opened her other eye.

The sound of pouring water seemed out of place. Was she imagining it?

"Tea?" Relic asked.

She struggled to sit up, her muscles painful and unyielding. She jerked one elbow under her chest and propped herself up for a moment. Then she swung her feet around and reached a seated position facing the small fire.

Relic set a plastic mug at her feet, tea bag dangling outside the lid. He scooped dirt onto the fire, smothering the last of it, then stood and disappeared around a bend in the cliffs.

Across the way, the landscape looked very different from last evening. The rigid stone fingers rose like specters in the early shadows, the sky above a pale, cloudless blue. Grass, sagebrush, and juniper were crocheted across the plateau like a hand-made blanket spread atop the bedrock.

She sipped on the strong, hot tea and thought about her captors.

Did the kidnappers want to catch her again, to collect a ransom? Or had it become even more serious than that?

She'd peered down the cliff that she and Relic had climbed to get away, down toward the spot where they'd seen a deputy and another man enter the alcove. The man must have been one of the kidnappers. Maybe the deputy was one of them, too. Were they chasing her now to capture her again or to kill her?

She set the mug in the dust and squeezed it until her hand stopped shaking. A gentle dawn began to warm the quilted plateau.

Was her friend, Sheila, okay? Sure she was; she must be. Sheila had been on the dance floor when the men had drugged Malia. Did Sheila wonder what happened to her? Or would Sheila leave her, just like she'd left the dead fawn in the park, the one she'd hit with her mother's car? Would Sheila even be looking for her?

Well, no one would ever find her here. Wherever here is.

A speck of doubt niggled in her brain, surprising her. Would Sheila really look for her? How hard would she try?

Relic returned to their little camp and sat across from her. "How are you today?" He'd pulled his ponytail tightly against his head and combed out his wiry goatee, some sort of desert cave man. His eyes were so dark they blended into his pupils, deep as the night sky, but there was concern in them, too, and she wanted to tell him her troubles.

"Thank you again, for everything. I guess I slept all right."

"Snored like a bear," his lips curled in a wide smile.

"Really?" She wrinkled her nose.

"Yep."

"Well…"

"So why are those baboons after you?"

She told him more about that night at the bar with Sheila; the music, drinks, lights, the guys who came to her and shot her with a needle full of something. Waking up in the old camper trailer and panicking.

Relic asked: "You said you went there with a friend? Is she okay?"

"I sure hope so." She stared at the ground. "Sheila's amazing, really, a big social influencer all through Los Angeles County."

Relic's squinted, confusion on his face. "Social influenza?"

"What? No, no. Influencer."

"What's that?"

"How long have you been out here? In this wilderness?"

"Not long enough."

"An influencer is someone who influences others."

"I figured that much. She influences them how?"

"She has her own insta—"

"Insta?"

"—gram and podcast. They're social media platforms, ways to get your opinions out to others, out to the public."

"What's her area of expertise?"

"What? No, it's not like that, it's just her thoughts about news of the day or what other people are doing or saying."

"Gossip."

"No, not gossip." She thought for a moment. "Well, sometimes. But mostly it's information and reactions to things."

"So, someone with lots of opinions can be an influencer?"

"Yes."

"But no expertise in the subjects she's influencing about?"

"Well…"

"Sounds more like social influenza to me. Spreads from person to person, like a virus."

"Hmmph." This sasquatch has no idea, she thought.

"But you like your friend anyway, right?"

"Sure, I do. I'd like to be more like her, too. She has a great sense of fashion, so yes, my pants and top," she pointed at her chest, "are what she recommended. And I just got a haircut like hers." She touched her curls.

"You must really admire her."

"No, I…" She thought for a moment. "Well, maybe."

Relic narrowed his eyes, watching her. "You almost want to be her."

She rubbed the bottom of the mug in the sand at her feet, staring at it, a realization dawning. Sasquatch was partially right. She didn't just admire Sheila; she wanted to live Sheila's life. She wanted to be influential and popular. Who wouldn't? More cash to spend, parties for fun, men to flirt with. Sasquatch didn't understand it at all, and he didn't seem to like Sheila even though he knew nothing about her. Well, except what Malia had told him. Damn it. What the hell does he know, anyway? Warm blotches formed on her neck, and her mind shut like a vault. She was done talking about it.

CHAPTER 30

Teddy felt a bead of sweat roll down his side. He'd cooked scrambled eggs and coffee for breakfast, heating the kitchen, and the morning sun was already baking the camper. Cooper sat on the couch in the RV, staring out the window, knees bouncing, buttocks shifting.

"I can't just sit here anymore." Cooper stood and slid his hand across his bald scalp. "I'm gonna hike back up the creek bed to the spot where it turns up the canyon. See if I can see Reed or the deputy from there."

"I thought you weren't too crazy about hiking."

"I'm not going far. And no big backpacks today, just a little one for water."

"Right." Teddy cranked open a window. "Damn hot inside here anyway."

Cooper squeezed past him and went into a bedroom down the narrow hall. Teddy took a seat on the couch, folding his hands in front of him.

Cooper returned, a daypack on his back, Glock in a shoulder holster. "Stay here, okay? In case they come back a different way."

"Okay."

"If they do, come get me. I won't go too far, maybe a mile or two. If I don't see them, I'll come back. Before it gets dark."

"Right. Good luck, boss."

Cooper stopped and looked at Teddy, blue eyes searching Teddy's face like a spotlight in the night. What was Cooper thinking? Was he worried that Teddy was losing faith in him, or doubting his plan?

Teddy squirmed in his seat. "What?"

"Nothing. Just thinking." He gave his head a quick, sideways shake and turned for the front door. "Don't do anything stupid while I'm gone."

Teddy felt his face warm.

Cooper slammed the door on his way out, the sound of his boots fading in the distance.

"Don't do anything stupid while I'm gone," Teddy mimicked Cooper's voice in a nasal tone. In his normal voice, he said: "How about I don't do anything stupid while you're here?"

Teddy stood and paced the hallway, up to the main bedroom, back to the couch, and back again.

What should he do? His grandmother had once told him to start with what he knew for sure, then figure it out from there.

He knew that the girl's father was not going to pay a ransom without proof that they had her in custody. Maybe they could grab her again, maybe not. But now a deputy could identify him, Reed, and Cooper.

He also knew he didn't trust Reed. He knew Cooper was going to break his promise that no one would get hurt on this job. He knew Cooper had just taken his pistol with him to try to find Reed and the deputy. And the girl. So young. Cute, too. He knew he could not shoot, kill, or hurt her or even Deputy Dipshit. The officer had no idea who he'd teamed up with when Reed joined the hunt.

He had to bail.

He knew he'd reached a decision, and it helped him to calm down. He ran a finger along the kitchen countertop, pondering the girl's escape and also his own. Remembering the black pickup they'd driven to this remote spot, the RV, of course, and the deputy's truck. The pickup and RV were rented from a small business on Peacock Street in L.A., all paid for and legit. Well, there weren't a lot of businesses on Peacock Street that were legit, but a shady rental place was just what they'd needed.

Cooper had used a fake I.D. and paid in cash. No way to trace them back. Their original plan was to abandon both vehicles. Cooper had a local contact, someone who would loan them a car and later report it as stolen. By then, they'd be back in L.A. Probably burn up the car in some back alley.

Of course, the plan had included five million dollars in a ransom payout, split four ways. The bulk to Cooper, a little to his local pal, the rest to Teddy and Reed. Teddy's take? One full million. But that was another thing he knew for certain: there'd be no money at the end of this job anymore. And he wasn't sure what Cooper or Reed might do about that.

He pulled back the curtain and searched outside. Cooper was out of view, probably down in the dry creek bed by now. Shadows filled the arroyo and stretched behind the RV.

Didn't the sheriff say he was looking for a missing man? What was that all about? Did Cooper or Reed have anything to do with it?

He tapped his fingernails on the counter and decided the missing man was a side issue. Think about transportation, instead. He could take the black pickup. Leave the RV for Cooper and Reed. That way, they still had a way out, a way back to the highway. Cooper's friend could still slip them his car, get them away clean.

What about the deputy's vehicle? He could pull some wires, maybe remove the battery and hide it. Just something to slow whoever might try to follow him in it.

Where would he go?

Florida. He could drive east from here, maybe into Colorado or New Mexico by morning, then get rid of the pickup. Steal a car every 24 hours until he made it to the Sunshine State. He'd always wanted to check it out, fish on the gulf, snorkel in the sea, bum it on the beach. He'd ask around, find someone who could get him a fake driver's license there. Start over. But he'd need some cash.

He hurried to Cooper's bedroom and searched the drawers and the tiny closet for money, checking pockets in clothes and cubbies where a wallet might fit. He lifted the mattress and found a large, flat stack of hundreds along with a fat manila envelope. Inside the envelope, he saw more stacks of hundreds, maybe six thousand dollars in each stack. He ran his fingers along the outside, feeling at least ten stacks. Holy crap. He thought for a moment. Cooper had arranged for some outside help with this job and a safe car to get out of the State. Maybe this was the pay off money for that. Lots of cash, but a drop in the bucket if you think about the five-million-dollar ransom.

He closed the envelope and stuffed it back

into place.

Teddy's goal was to get the hell out before someone starting shooting, not to rip off the boss. And not to leave him stranded, without a getaway car. After all, Cooper had been a friend of sorts. Took him on this job, even though it had turned to shit. Teddy owed him something, at least. Maybe he'd even leave him a short letter, so he wouldn't get too mad. Maybe they'll cross paths again one day.

And he didn't want Reed scouring the country to find him and inflict some kind of revenge. Reed was just the kind of guy to do that, too.

He counted a total of five thousand dollars in the flat stack, loose travelling money, and took half. He wasn't going to leave Cooper with nothing.

He gathered soda and sandwiches from the refrigerator and scribbled a quick note. He anchored it to the table with a container of mustard. He grabbed the keys to the truck and looked out the window again, the pit of his stomach twisting.

All clear.

Teddy ran out the door.

CHAPTER 31

"Hold out your hands." Relic moved closer to her.

Malia lifted her palms upward and he poured rounded objects, blue, green, red, into the cup her fingers made.

"What's this?"

"Breakfast."

"Really?" She realized they were peanut M&M's and tossed two into her mouth.

He set a half-empty water bottle by her feet. "This'll be yours as we hike today. Sip it as we go. Don't guzzle."

She nodded, luxuriating in the taste of warm milk chocolate. Why did it taste so especially wonderful out here?

Relic had explained that they had miles to hike today to reach a small spring where they could replenish their water. From there, they'd hike down a side canyon then back toward Star Chart Ruins, where she'd been held in the camper, and to the dirt road to the highway. They'd have to avoid the kidnappers, but Relic thought that would be easy and it was the closest option for getting her to safety.

She swallowed the last of the peanut candies in her hand, already nostalgic about them. Relic had better have some more of these.

Relic shouldered his pack and stepped away from their temporary camp. He'd tossed the fire ring rocks across the ground and buried the ashes so well she could hardly tell they'd spent the night here.

She leaned down, picked up the water bottle, and slowly took a couple of steps, her muscles tight as rubber bands. Her joints felt like each one had its own version of a throbbing toothache and she imagined gristle scraping over gristle with every movement. She touched her pocket, another involuntary reach for a phone that wasn't there. Games. Boys. News. Fashion's latest. All gone.

Relic was way ahead of her already, so she put her head down and pushed a little faster. They climbed a large, barren rock and by the time they stopped at the top, her ankles ached from climbing up the angled slope. Relic searched the area for a moment. They scooted down the other side, her shoes slipping against the smooth stone.

An expanse of sage and grass opened before them

and Relic settled into a steady rhythm. She couldn't keep up, but he stopped every so often to wait for her.

What would she have done without him?

The ground rose and fell in shallow swells, and they seemed to be following a thin trail of some sort, weaving around stones and cacti. Her throat seemed to harden in the dry air, so she stopped and took a quick drink. Oh, how she wanted more! Just another one, for now. Or an icy margarita. Or a sundae with fudge and caramel and cherries and bananas.

God, she was hungry; so starved she thought she'd collapse. She took a full breath and forced herself to move forward, step, step, step. After a while, she fell into a new sort of rhythm, the yearning slipping slowly away, like untying the knot of a bad dream. She hadn't spent this much time outdoors in years, maybe ever. The air was so clear it seemed she'd been transported to another planet, a fantasy landscape filled with the sweet, earthy scent of sage and fine dust.

They stopped on a small rise and Relic rationed more M&M's. After a quick drink, her water bottle was virtually empty.

He's a quiet man, she thought, and she didn't mind. Her urge to talk had dampened under the task at hand. She became aware of shadows cast by the rocks and grass, an afternoon slipping later into the day.

Relic pulled binoculars from his pack and lay on the ground, scanning the distance. She sat next to him, looking across the plateau.

Silently, he handed the binoculars to her and pointed. She raised them to her eyes and searched the horizon.

"To the left," he said.

She adjusted the focus and kept looking until a flash caught her attention. She tried to steady the binoculars.

Holy shit. Her heart began to pound. Two men were winding their way up a ridge several miles from her. One of them wore a police-style uniform.

The kidnappers.

She lowered the binoculars and stared at Relic.

"Yep," he said.

"One of them is the cop."

"Yep."

"Will they find us?"

"Maybe. They're going north, though, and we're going southeast. I don't think they've found our trail. And if they do, it will take them to our camp, farther north."

"I've been wondering about this. Why would the police be one of the kidnappers? Or be helping them?"

Relic stroked his goatee. "I know that deputy."

"You do?"

"Chased me a couple of times. Blamed me, I think, for some trouble out here."

"So, he's crooked?"

"No. Well, I don't know for sure. But it's possible he doesn't know you were kidnapped. He might think he's searching for a criminal. Someone who ran when he chased after her."

"But—"

"Yep. Not fair, not right." He lifted himself onto his elbows and backed away from the ridge.

"When I go for help, well, what do I do now? Can I trust the local sheriff to help me?"

Relic thought for a moment, put his hand to his forehead, and pressed.

CHAPTER 32

Stanovich put the Jeep in park and scanned the area. A 1960's style house, red brick with a low roof, anchored the end of the road. A lonely patch of lawn grew under the front window, purple Salvia reaching up the wall. An addition to the place spread to the left, wood instead of brick, and beyond that were corrals and a large shed. Wire fencing went from the corner of the addition into a grove of box elders and out of sight. A wire gate led behind the house, their posts angled away from each other, threatening to fall to the ground.

He was here to see if Mrs. Rivers had recently seen or heard from Karl. Sheriff Leavitt said that Karl worked for her from time to time.

He slid from the Jeep and walked toward the front door. A cheap aluminum screen covered a metal door with no windows. He knocked loudly on the frame, announcing himself.

No one came to the door. He could hear no noises inside, or anywhere, so he moved to the edge of the addition, toward the tired gate.

A bay mare stood on the far side of a corral, resting a hoof, the horse half asleep. The wind had died into stillness.

He unlatched the gate, and it fell forward a bit, so he swiveled through, lifted it back into place, and locked it there. He hooked his thumbs in his belt and moved along the outside wall of the addition, searching for signs of human life in the side yard. The shed out back had weathered, vertical boards with a metal roof. Its door was closed. He reached the edge of the addition.

A pair of round metal cylinders appeared before his face, gray and hollow, edging closer to his nose.

"Damn!" He leapt back, arms twirling.

The double-barreled shotgun stayed where it was.

A woman in jeans and red cotton shirt had her cheek pressed against the stock, one eye squinted nearly shut, a hard edge in the steel blue eye that was open.

"Hey!" Stanovich raised his arms in the air.

"Sorry." The woman lowered the shotgun.

"You could kill someone with that!"

"That's the idea, bud, but I didn't know you were a deputy."

Stanovich touched his hand to his chest.

"You should announce yourself next time you decide to sneak onto someone's property."

"I did; I knocked on the door—"

"Didn't hear you announce," she interrupted, giving him no credit for the attempt.

Stanovich adjusted his hat. "Are you Mrs. Mable Rivers?"

"The one and only."

"I'm here because we're looking for a man, Karl, uh…" suddenly, he'd forgotten Karl's last name.

She pointed the barrel at the ground. "What's wrong with Karl?"

"Maybe nothing, just…some of his friends say he's been missing now, for nearly three days and we're checking with anyone who may have seen him or heard from him."

"Karl doesn't have any friends." She canted her head, the observation a statement of fact.

"Well, Mrs. Rivers, a couple of people have said he's missing."

"Hell, yeah, he's missing. Supposed to fix my front gate, the one you snuck through. Bought new gateposts and everything and the man has disappeared."

"Yes, that's what I mean, he's disappeared."

She nodded, unimpressed with his interrogation skills.

"When was the last time you saw him?"

She looked to the sky, as if for the answer. "Eight days ago."

"Oh. Do you have any idea where he might be now?"

"I don't keep track of that man." Her head moved from side to side, emphasizing each word as she went.

"Okay."

"When you find the slacker, tell him he owes me a new gate."

They stared at each other for a moment.

"Yes, Mrs. Rivers. I'll be sure to do that." He hesitated. "And next time, maybe don't point that thing at your local law enforcement."

"Maybe don't sneak up on a woman like that, next time."

"Yes, ma'am."

CHAPTER 33

Cooper had gone up the arroyo again, nervous energy driving him there, but he hadn't seen Reed or the deputy. He'd shouted Reed's name several times but heard no reply. He'd hidden the satellite phone in his knapsack because reception was the same out in the open, maybe better, than it was in the big RV and he needed to make another call to the girl's father. After staring up the canyon for a while, he finally shrugged and turned back along the dry creek bed.

He found a flat rock to sit on and stared at his boots, thinking about the call he was about to make. He needed to keep Manning focused. And he needed to get him to the next step: instructions for how to make the ransom payment. He pulled a note from his pocket with bitcoin account numbers on it. He dialed the satellite phone and waited for the distinctive click when someone answered. He held the voice modulator to his larynx.

"Manning?" Cooper sounded like a robot.

Static.

"Manning?"

"Who is this?"

"The man who has your daughter."

"Why are you doing this?" Manning asked.

"Why do you think? You have until ten in the morning on Monday to make the payment or you'll never see your daughter alive again."

Manning was silent.

"You hear me?"

"Yes."

Cooper read the account number from his note. "Transfer must be done by ten. Got it?"

"I still don't understand what you think you're doing!"

"Don't piss me off, Manning."

"What proof do I have that…that anyone should pay this?"

Cooper shifted his feet. Jeez this jerk's an ass. But maybe he was getting somewhere—Manning seemed to be asking for proof that his stepdaughter was still alive. "I have her purse, her driver's license, her credit cards."

"You're a real bastard, you know that?"

"She's safe and sound where no one will ever find

her. Fail to make your payment and she'll die of thirst, alone, locked away. Make your payment as instructed and you'll get directions to find her. Whether she dies or not is all up to you."

"You'd do that?"

"I'll walk away in a second and she'll die. But it will take days."

"This is a crazy ass call."

"I can show you crazy, Mr. Manning."

"What kind of man are you?"

Cooper's face reddened. "What do you think this is? Some kind of game show?"

"Prove to me that you really have her."

"I've given you all you need."

"What if I don't think so?"

"Is that a chance you want to take?"

The line went quiet.

"You hear me, Manning?"

"Yes."

Cooper disconnected. Manning was turning out to be a real ass-wipe. But the call had been a little better this time—at least the man hadn't hung up mid-sentence. But he'd moaned and groaned about Cooper like an un-happy internet customer rather than a man being black-mailed into paying a ransom. Cooper had given him the payment instructions, though, so that was progress. Still, Manning's reactions were a little odd. If it were Cooper, he'd be asking for more time, asking for further instructions, worried and panicked. Even if the girl wasn't his biological daughter, but a stepdaughter. Maybe he'd gotten some advice about how to handle the kidnapping. Maybe he'd been told to demand proof that Cooper had his stepdaughter in custody. Proof he didn't happen to have at the moment.

He'd make a call to Hanna for a quick update, then get himself back to the RV.

CHAPTER 34

Hanna had volunteered to clean the casita behind the main house on Saturday, in hopes of listening and learning more about Mr. Manning's reaction to the ransom call. Cooper had said the man might have hung up on him or they might have lost the signal. Hanna could see that Manning was distressed but why hadn't he agreed to pay up? Cooper hadn't even had the time to tell him where and how to make the payment and now Cooper was counting on her to find out why.

She'd asked Cooper to call Manning again at one o'clock today and she would make sure to be in the main residence when the call came in. She sprayed furniture polish on the cherry table and wiped it down.

She checked her phone. Almost time.

Hanna took a slow breath and wiped her hands on her smock. The casita was empty, an apartment-sized building for overnight guests. It had a four-burner gas stove, refrigerator, narrow kitchen island, and a seating area with a television and game center. One bathroom with a shower and one bedroom completed the unit. She'd give her right arm to afford a place as nice as this, and the Mannings used it only a few days out of the year. She'd finished cleaning but had left some rags and her sweeper in the living room at the main house as an excuse to go back there.

She walked the short distance to the side entrance of the house, taking her time, listening for anything to indicate that Mr. Manning had taken another call from Cooper.

No one was in the laundry room. Manning's home office was around the corner, so she moved in that direction. The hall was empty. Distant voices echoed through the foyer. She made her way toward the office and heard a phone ring inside.

Manning had answered, his voice gruff, upset.

She slid closer to the door, which was opened a crack.

"No," Manning had said, then something she couldn't make out. She could hear his footsteps pacing across the floor.

"Who is this?" he demanded.

She glanced around for signs of anyone else in the house.

He grumbled something into the phone.

A sound made her jump. Manning's wife was coming directly toward her. Hanna rubbed her hands on her smock and hurried away, toward the sweeper in the living room. She grabbed the vacuum and slid her eyes back toward the wife, worried she'd been discovered.

Manning banged out of his office, the sound like an electric jolt to her nerves. She gripped the handle until her knuckles were white.

"Damn it!" Manning threw his arms in the air. His wife looked worried, harried. She approached him now, her hands outstretched as if to calm the man, but he rushed past, cursing now, and she followed closely behind.

Out of earshot.

She rolled the unplugged vacuum down the hall, hoping to hear the conversation, but the couple had moved through the living room and up the stairs. She dared not follow up there.

She returned to the casita and plugged in the sweeper, her hands shaking.

When her cell phone rang, she jumped, hand to her chest. "Cooper?" she asked.

"Yeah, what's Manning's reaction? Could you hear or see anything?"

"He and his wife are really pissed. Really upset, I'd say."

"What about the ransom? Did he talk about that? How to pay up?"

"I couldn't tell about that, sorry. I barely got what I could before they both ran upstairs."

"So, why isn't he telling me he's making payment arrangements? The guy just flies off the handle and hangs up."

Hanna leaned into the living room, looking and listening. She thought about the old kidnapping, the one that had gone so smoothly for Cooper a few years ago. "Maybe it is because he's just the stepdad. Maybe he and his stepdaughter *hate* each other."

"Maybe."

"Maybe his wife is pushing him to pay and he's against it? Maybe they're in a big fight about it, I mean, five million dollars could really hurt them, even bankrupt them. Or maybe he hasn't told his wife the truth."

"Still…you'd think he'd be asking me to give him time to work it out, time to arrange for the payment."

Hanna stepped back into the hallway. "Maybe he's having money problems. Maybe he can't raise that much money. Some of these really rich guys are actually up to their necks in debt."

"Maybe it's all those things. But you did say he's

pissed off?"

"Clearly, yes, very unhappy."

"So maybe he's just in a *panic* about it all."

"He's really worked up, that's for sure."

"Well, keep hanging around. Call me if you get any more intel."

She nodded, glancing into the living room again. "I won't be here on the job tomorrow. It's Sunday. But I'll be back on Monday."

"Okay, we figured this might take until Monday or Tuesday to get it wrapped up. You did great, babe. It does sound like he's in a panic right now, trying to figure out what to do, maybe in the middle of a big fight with the wife. He'll get past it. Just stay chill and we'll be done with this soon."

"I hope so."

"Quick enough, we'll be paying for someone else to clean our place."

She smiled.

CHAPTER 35

Her legs were so tired they were numb. Her torso seemed to float across the ground like an apparition, the aches in her hips, calves, and ankles, pushed into the recesses of her mind. They'd walked another hour or so and dusk was settling on the plateau, casting sepia tones over rock and brush. The ground dropped below her, lowering into a curve that took them closer to a side canyon, a maw in the rugged earth, split wide open. Cliffs stood like sentinel walls a quarter of a mile away. The curve in front of them continued, lowering even farther, and ended at the base of a rocky outcrop. Relic trotted ahead and began clearing space near the low sandstone bluff.

How did he still have any energy?

She shuffled closer and he pointed to the ground. She could barely bend her knees and once she did, she fell quickly into the sand and lay flat in the dust, staring into a blushing sky.

"I'll go find firewood," he said.

She raised her hand in acknowledgement and let it fall back across her chest. She couldn't take another day of his. She'd have to tell Relic. They'd have to stay here and recover. Relic could go for help, bring a helicopter back or something. Leave her some M&M's.

Quiet filled the little alcove and her breathing settled out. The air cooled gently, and a quick shiver ran through her.

Here she was. In the middle of nowhere, being chased by cops and kidnappers. What had she done to deserve this? Go out with her friend for a drink? What was Sheila doing now? Did she worry about her? Was her friend out there searching for her?

Worry wriggled its way into a crack in her mind, expanding like winter ice in a fissure. Was she even thinking about what mattered most to her?

Something clicked and she had the thought that Sheila wouldn't worry at all, not past the first question: "where the hell did Malia go?" Sheila would move on right away, on to the next drink or dance or guy she fancied. It rattled her that she thought that about her friend. That maybe she wasn't that much of a friend at all, even after she'd defended her to Relic. She missed her older sister, Anne, now more than ever, but in some ways, she'd moved on. Maybe it was time for Malia to move on, too. Or maybe it wasn't.

She was just too tired to think straight, that was it.

Something rustled in the grass near her feet and static electricity seemed to fill her lungs.

It wasn't Relic.

She lifted her head slowly, just a little. A large, brown body stood nearby, its head turned away from her and it felt like a banshee had risen in the center of her chest, stealing her breath.

What the hell?

She clamped her eyes shut, squeezed against her brow. *Play dead, play dead.* That's all she could think of, all she could really do, anyway.

The beast shuffled a bit and seemed to plop at her feet.

Steaming lava seemed to pulse through her heart, out to her arms, hands, feet, dissipating in the cool breeze.

Nothing happened.

She opened one eye.

The animal continued to face away from her, its back as large as Malia herself and muscled, its hairy hide thatched in grays, blacks, and browns.

What the hell is that thing? And where the hell is Relic?

CHAPTER 36

Cooper stomped his boots outside the RV and opened the door.

"Teddy?" He walked inside. A single light in the kitchen made the room feel smaller, almost claustrophobic. "Teddy!" He flicked on another light.

The sun had crossed below the horizon maybe thirty minutes ago, ambient light now fully lost to the night sky. He'd trudged about two miles up the arroyo and waited in case Reed or the deputy came back, then gave up and returned to the camper. He'd seen no sign of them. He hoped they were hot on the trail of the girl and the man with the ponytail.

He took a cold beer from the refrigerator and plopped onto the couch. After two long pulls, he listened for any sound from Teddy or anything else. The RV was as silent as a coffin.

A tub of mustard sat on the corner of the kitchen

table, left out of the refrigerator. He'd missed it when he first arrived. He lifted himself from the couch with a grunt and went to the bottle. Beneath was a note from Teddy.

"Ahhh…shit."

Cooper pulled the paper from under the mustard and read it quickly first, then slowly, mouthing the words as he went:

I know what you and Reed are planning. You broke your promise. I want nothing to do with it. I'm taking the truck, but you can drive the RV out of here. You're not stuck here. Don't try to call me again. No more jobs with you and Reed. I took the battery out of the deputy's truck so if he comes back, he can't follow you. (I hid it in the creek bed.) – Teddy.

Damn it. He should have known Teddy would do something stupid. He smacked the tabletop with the flat of his hand and swore. He took another deep drink of beer and stared at the ceiling.

A thought struck him, and he ran to the bedroom, tossing blankets and bed sheets aside. He lifted the mattress and checked the manila envelope full of cash. It all seemed to be there. He counted the loose stack of hundreds that lay next to the envelope. Half of that cash was missing. His cheeks warmed, his fingers shook, anger rising and then it plateaued, and he stood there, confused. Why hadn't Teddy taken all of it?

He placed the mattress down and straightened the sheets, thinking. Teddy had taken what he needed but left the rest for him and Reed. More importantly, he'd left the envelope of cash needed for the getaway car. Teddy had run away like a coward, but he'd tried to be fair about it. Sort of. Cooper walked back into the living room, feeling slightly better, then angry again, then a bit confused about it all.

Teddy was gone, but, he thought, Teddy had already played his part in the kidnapping. Maybe it was all right. With Teddy in the wind, it might even be easier for Cooper and Reed to disappear someplace, maybe north, into Idaho. They had the RV, like the note said, to get them to the highway. And to the escape car.

When Reed gets back, we'll just drive on out of here.

This "job," as Teddy called it, was starting to turn to shit. Manning was a stubborn fool who was dragging his feet. Reed was going to have to kill the deputy at least, not much doubt about that.

It was time to confirm they could still get the hell out of here. He lifted the satellite phone from his daypack and dialed.

"What's up?"

"This is Cooper. Manning has his payment instructions, but we've hit a snag. We want to be ready to fly on out of here."

"Tell me."

"When we made the first ransom call, the father hung up on us, like he didn't give a shit. He was squirrely on the second call, too. Can't explain it. Some hiker dude helped the girl escape. Reed will take care of it, then we're out of here. Sometime Sunday."

"That's not my problem. We have a deal."

"Yes, yes, the rest of your payment. Just help keep us safe in the meantime and get us that other vehicle."

"When?"

"Tomorrow night, late. Maybe Monday."

"A half mile from the highway, there's a trench. Just off the dirt road and out of sight. Leave the RV and the black pickup there and walk to the pavement." Cooper saw no need to tell his contact that Teddy had run off with the black truck. "An older model station wagon style Ford will be waiting by the side of the road. Key will be on top of the driver side front tire."

"Stolen?"

"Won't be reported for 48 hours."

"Good. Your final payment——are you sure we can't just send it to you through bitcoin?"

"I told you I don't know anything about that crap."

"Then, where can we leave it?"

"There's a small cairn—rocks piled as a trail marker—below the speed limit sign. The Ford will be parked just a few feet away from it. Put it under the rocks."

"Pleasure doing business with you."

"If payment isn't there, the whole county and the damned FBI will know what you're driving and the license plate number."

"Okay, okay. Jeez, man." Cooper ran a hand across his bald pate and hung up the phone. He took another swig of beer. At least he still had twenty-five hundred dollars for the cost of getting out of here.

CHAPTER 37

Malia tensed. Brush was being dragged across the ground, then stopped.

"Mae." Relic's words were soft and friendly.

She opened her eyes and dared to roll her head to the left.

"You've made a new friend," Relic began pulling branches toward their little camp.

"What…is it?" her words sputtered like a choking engine.

"It?" He laid the wood on the ground. "That's Mae."

The animal turned its head toward Malia, coffee-colored eyes rimmed with black, a natural mascara, slanted upward like an Egyptian Queen. The fur across her cheek was lighter than the rest, her mouth a small line of dark beneath a charcoal nose that glistened with moisture. Her ears rotated on her head like antennae, huge, soft, fuzzy. Whitened follicles reached outward from the center of her ears like an unkempt beard.

"It looks so big. Is it a Moose?"

"A *Moose*? No, no, no. She's a doe. A girl deer."

"Oh, yeah, yeah, of course."

The deer stared at Malia, and Malia at the deer.

"Holy shit."

"Yeah, she's a beauty, isn't she?" Relic gathered stones, placing them near the back of the alcove.

"What's she doing here? Is she dangerous?" Her voice squeaked.

"She lives here, of course."

"She just comes up to us?"

"Well, it took her a while to get used to me." He moved slowly toward her and the doe stretched her neck toward him. He scratched above her nose and her eyes closed, enjoying the moment.

Malia pulled her feet away from Mae and sat up quietly.

"She's a curious one. Came up to me a couple of years ago. Took a while to gain her trust, you know."

Malia nodded. Relic continued to scratch Mae's forehead.

"How…?"

"Amazing, huh?"

"No shit."

Relic moved away from Mae and to his pack, where he pulled out several items, rummaging through the bottom. He lifted a pack of something, opened it, and poured it onto the back of his hand. He returned it to his pack and walked back to Mae, his hand extended.

The deer stayed on the ground and leaned toward him, licking his fingers, her tongue wet and pointed.

Relic said, "Salt."

She finished licking, and Relic rubbed above her nose again. "Want to give her a scratch?"

"Uh…"

"Just move slowly, reach out." Relic stood back and watched.

Would the deer have some kind of germs, or bugs, or lice or something on her? But her fur looked so clean. And Relic had just touched her.

Malia caught her bottom lip with her teeth and leaned forward slowly. She and Mae gazed into each other's eyes, drawn together. Her fingers touched the fur on Mae's nose, then slid to her cheek and Mae pushed her head into Malia's hand, rubbing against it, feeling its heat, its comfort.

She was petting a wild animal, a deer on the plateau, a warm, living being that reacted to her touch like a loving mate, a fellow mammal. Mae's chest rose and fell with each breath, releasing a brief snort and Malia pulled away, still staring into those intelligent, haunting eyes.

Her mind flashed on the city park with Sheila, the little fawn lying dead in the grass, and Sheila's reaction: "It's just a dumb animal."

Something fell open in Malia's gut, a door blown off its hinges.

CHAPTER 38

Dawson stopped, hands on his hips, and scanned the eastern ridge, working his way to the west. They'd criss-crossed the plateau all day and seen no trail, no sign of the ponytailed man or the girl he was with.

"We're going to have to camp tonight." Dawson pointed at the last vestige of light on the horizon. "There's a knoll over there that might give us some shelter." He looked back at Reed, who was also searching the landscape.

"Yeah," the man dropped his chin to his chest.

They were exhausted.

"We'll need water tomorrow. I can take us to a spring I've seen on the maps," Dawson pointed west. "We can replenish there."

Reed took a breath and began walking toward the knoll and Dawson followed him. Once there, they set a light tarp on the leeward side of the hill and Dawson strode out into the dark, the flashlight sweeping ahead of him. He found a few errant branches of sage and juniper, gathering them in his arms. Reed watched as Dawson dropped them several feet from the tarp and arranged a small fire.

Reed searched through the pack that Cooper had brought to them and found two cans of stew and two beers.

"Your friend put canned food into that pack?" Dawson asked.

"I had no idea."

"Glad *you* carried that, and not me," Dawson said.

"I wouldn't have if I'd have known."

"Well, I'm glad for the brews, though," Dawson blew on the fire and added wood.

They heated the stew and shoveled the food into their mouths, spoons and tin cans clinking like cowbells. "What else you got in there?" Dawson asked.

Reed fished around in the pack and pulled out a flashlight, first aid kit, poncho, and bag of cookies.

"How about that beer now and a chocolate chip?" Dawson asked.

"You bet, officer."

"Call me Dawson."

A half-smile formed on his lips then disappeared. "Okay."

Firelight glanced off Reed's cheeks, shadows stretching down his face and under his neck. He looked at Dawson, boring into his pupils like a pair of drill bits, then slacked off quickly when he realized Dawson was staring back. Something was just under the surface with that man, Dawson thought, some kind of subterranean truth. What was it?

Reed smiled and handed Dawson a beer and the bag of cookies.

"Where are you guys from, again?" Dawson asked.

"L.A."

"Your friends, too?"

"Yeah."

"Hunters?"

"Well, we like to think so." Reed took a long swallow of beer.

Dawson nodded. "When do you guys head back home?"

Reed's eyes narrowed, then opened again. "Not sure. What day is it?"

"Saturday night."

"Will your sheriff join us out here soon?" Reed asked.

"He should. Tomorrow, at the latest, I'd say mid-day."

Reed nodded and stared into the fire.

"We could use his help." Dawson added. He took another drink, put a cookie in his pocket, and handed the bag back to Reed.

"For sure."

"I still can't figure out why in the hell those two – the man and the young woman – are out here. What would they be doing here?"

"Beats me." Reed shook his head.

"And it seems like they were in that old trailer."

"Camping out? Maybe?"

"So, why wreck the trailer? And why run away from us?" Dawson scratched his neck.

Reed kept his eyes on the ground and shrugged.

Silence unspooled between them.

"What do you do for a living, Mr. Reed?"

"Friends just call me Reed."

Dawson nodded.

"I'm an insurance underwriter. I work on contracts and manage a team of salesmen."

"Oh." Like hell, Dawson thought.

"I work out in the gym," he said, as if to explain how an office nerd could be in such good shape. "Three days a week." He moved his arms up and down, imitating the lift of barbells. "Can't let the job turn me into a desk jockey."

"Yeah." The man moved more like a boxer than a desk jockey. Dawson felt a knot working its way up his diaphragm.

"I'm beat, deputy. I think I'm going to get some rest." His lips flashed a thin smile.

"Yeah, I agree. We'll be up at dawn with a lot of ground to cover." He crumpled the empty beer can and stuffed it into the pack, watching Reed from the corner of his eye.

"Right." Reed smirked for just a second, the look as crude and transient as a bubble of snot.

CHAPTER 39

Mae rose to her knees then stood as Relic and Malia watched. She turned and hopped away from the camp and quickly out of sight.

"She's a bit shy of fire, of course." Relic stacked the wood he'd gathered, breaking some into smaller pieces. He built a quick fire-ring, like he'd done last night, and soon had a small blaze lighting the area.

Mae had left little heart-shaped prints in the dust.

"Will she come back?"

"Maybe. After the fire's out."

"She's like…some sort of pet?"

"Pet?" His brow squeezed down on his eyes. "Hardly."

"Oh."

"Maybe I'm *her* pet."

"She's…?"

"She lives in this area. I see her a few times a year. I share my salt with her, and she shares her company with me."

"She was a complete surprise."

"Surprises re-adjust our thinking. And our thinking is what channels our actions."

"Yeah…"

Relic handed her two pieces of jerky. "This is supper tonight. And I refilled our water at the spring around the bend."

Her mouth watered like it had a mind of its own, and she wrestled her first bite from the dried meat. Relic pulled a small bottle from his pack and took a swig. He sat cross-legged in front of the fire.

"Want some?"

"What is it?" She took the plastic flask from his hand.

"Homemade hooch."

"Oh." She finished swallowing the jerky and took a quick shot. "Smooth," she coughed.

"Slight taste of peach this year."

"Yeah." And gasoline, she thought. But after it settled in her stomach, she took another drink.

"Do you work at a job?" he asked.

"I'm a student. Business school."

"What do you study in business school?"

"Finance Analytics. Accounting. Entrepreneurship."

"Do you like it?"

"No, not really." Her own answer surprised her. "It's just that…" Sheila took those classes, and she wanted to hang out with Sheila.

"You don't find the study of money to be a fascinating subject?"

She smiled. "Well, you can make some serious money in the right business."

"What do you do with all that money you make?"

"Spend it, of course."

"On what?"

"Whatever I want."

"You should be suspicious of what you want."

"Oh?"

"You'd spend it on yourself, then."

"Well, yes."

"Is money the means to an end or an end itself?"

He sounded like a philosophy professor, she thought. "The means, I guess. The pursuit of happiness."

"It's not the pursuit of happiness that counts, but the happiness of the pursuit."

"Oh." Now he sounded like a damned greeting card writer. But she could see what he meant. She took another swig of the homemade gin and handed the flask back to him. The first drink was a little rough, the second one okay, but the third was smooth as silk.

"If you enjoy studying money, and making it, then more power to you, as they say."

"If I don't?"

"Then knock it off." He grinned.

"Yeah," she ran her finger in the dust. Now he sounded entirely practical.

"Be careful. Chasing greed is a race you'll never win."

"So, you're saying we need more of this," she waved her hand at the night sky. "*Nature?*"

"No. We need a shift in our point of view. 'Nature' is a word that divides us from it." He took a breath. "I get it – I use the word, too. But we're all made of the same stuff. Like Mae. We are born. We have families. We have joy, we have pain. Mae lost a fawn two years ago. She was grieving and I could see it. She came into my camp every night for a week after that. I like to think I was some comfort to her."

"Really?"

"Yep. We are curious about the world and why we're in it. But nature is not something that's out there, different from us, walled off from us. We are it and it is us."

"Touching Mae like that was…"

"Yep. Don't I know it."

CHAPTER 40

It had been a long, hot day. Stanovich brushed the dust from his cowboy hat and entered the main room of the Sheriff's Department. Grace left the dispatcher's office and followed him in. She sat in the chair behind Dawson's desk.

Sheriff Leavitt leaned on one edge of a credenza, chewing his lip.

Stanovich went to his own desk, pulled his chair out, and plopped into it. He nodded to each of them in turn.

"Any luck with Mrs. Rivers?" the sheriff asked.

"About got my face shot off."

Leavitt chuckled. "Sorry about that. Should've warned you about her. Keeps that shotgun with her like it's attached to her hip."

"Hell, yeah."

"Did she know where Karl might be?"

"Nope." Stanovich turned in his chair, the metal swivel squeaking. "She hasn't seen or heard from him in more than a week."

"I thought he was working at her place," Grace leaned forward.

"A few weeks back he repaired the fencing around her gate, and he was supposed to fix the gate, too, but it's still about to fall to the ground."

Sheriff Leavitt crossed his arms, a brown bear unhappy with its cubs.

"But I can try the Holly place later," Stanovich turned, metal grinding under his seat.

"Well, I, for one, am out of ideas." Grace released a breath. "How could he disappear like this?"

"Relatives out of state maybe?" Stanovich's chair squealed again as he shifted.

"Oil that damn thing, will you?" Leavitt grumbled.

"Sure."

"Do we know about any out of state relatives?" Grace asked.

Stanovich watched the sheriff. Some sort of tension filled the space, a vague discomfort that seemed to expand beyond their fears about the well-being of the missing man.

The sheriff turned his eyes to Stanovich and waited. He met the sheriff's gaze for a bit, then looked at the floor, wondering what his boss was thinking. He fidgeted in his seat and the chair squeaked again.

"Sorry." He stopped.

"It's been years since Karl worked at the mine, but maybe he gave them a next-of-kin designation." The sheriff released his arms and pointed at Grace. "See if you can get that. Any record like that and follow up. Reach out to whoever you find. At this point, it's fair to tell them he's missing."

"Yes, sir."

The sheriff nodded toward Stanovich. "You go to the Holly place and check if anyone there has any ideas."

"Yes, sir," Stanovich nodded. "Want me to go back to Slickrock Canyon or anyplace else, to check again?"

The sheriff's brow lifted. "Slickrock? Why Slickrock?"

Grace straightened her back.

"Or Moonshine Mesa, or any of the side canyons. Want me to double check any of those places?" He rolled the chair a little closer to his desk, a tactical retreat of sorts. Why did Slickrock seem to alarm the sheriff? He wished he hadn't mentioned it.

Sheriff Leavitt rapped Dawson's desk with his

knuckles, frustration, and maybe something else, coursing through him. "No. We don't have the manpower to keep checking the same places over and over again." He looked up at Stanovich. "Just check the Holly place then get back here and stay on your usual duties."

Stanovich spun, his chair complaining yet again.

The sheriff's eyes rolled toward the ceiling. "And grease that damn thing, will you?"

CHAPTER 41

She hadn't eaten oatmeal since she was a child and now she remembered why. But her hunger was as deep and cavernous as ever and the bland, pasty stuff had eased the ache. She thanked Relic and watched as he spread the fire ring around the area and buried the ashes from their little fire. Mae left last night and had not returned.

Relic placed a water bottle at her feet. "Take a big drink now then little sips as we cross the plateau."

The morning sun seemed to slide an auburn glaze across the landscape, a dimmable light bulb slowly turning up the intensity. The sage was olive-green, patches of grass a muted lime. A half mile away, burnished sandstone rose in a giant dome, the balding top of an earthen skull.

She took a long drink and stood slowly, her muscles stiff as wire. "How far do we need to go today?"

"About six miles."

She groaned.

Relic reached into his pack and handed her a bag of peanut M&M's and she quickly forgave him for the breakfast of lukewarm, tasteless, mush.

He shouldered his pack and scanned the horizon.

She watched him for a moment, pondering what and who this man was. He'd just given her his best trail food—a man whose most valuable property in the entire world was probably his batch of chocolate covered peanuts.

"We'll cross the plateau," he pointed, "and then we'll reach a side canyon there with steep walls, but a trail that will take us down to the valley and the dry creek. From there, we go back up creek to Star Chart Ruins and the road to the highway."

"Sounds like a long hike."

He shrugged.

She put the candies in her pocket for later and nodded at him to show the way.

They trudged across the open ground, the air quickly heating under a clear sky. After a while, her muscles, though tired, limbered with the motion of the hike. Relic stopped on a regular basis for water and rest, and they acquired a certain rhythm, slowing on the inclines, speeding on the downhill sections, dodging rocks and cacti and sagebrush. They rested and ate the candied peanuts about midday then resumed their hike across the plateau. Once or twice, she thought she saw Mae in the distance, but she wasn't sure.

When the sun was at their backs and shadows began to grow, they came upon a tall jumble of rocks. A rim of sandstone cliff came into view maybe a quarter of a mile from them, a crease of darker rock marking the edge of a canyon.

Relic slid his pack to the ground. "We're almost where we want to camp for the night."

"Thank god."

"Let's rest here a bit then head to the rim of the side canyon. That's the one that will take us down to the arroyo, the dry creek bed."

She sat on a low rock and reached her hands to the ground, stretching her back.

"Hey, there's Mae," Relic nodded to his right. The doe stood about thirty yards away, ears twisting like little satellite dishes. She'd followed them all this way. Or maybe Relic had followed her.

Relic sat on a stone, pack between his legs, and began looking for something. Malia ate a few more M&M's and took a measured drink of water. She barely had enough for another swig.

A small pebble struck her arm, and she glanced at Relic, who'd tossed it at her. He made a deep "shushing" sound and held a finger to his lips, his eyes urgent, focused on the deer. Mae's ears had swiveled forward, her eyes on something just out of Malia's sight, to the right of Relic. Then the deer's body shifted downward, tail erect, knees bent, ready to flee.

Mae had seen something. And she didn't like it one little bit.

CHAPTER 42

Relic pointed at Mae and Malia watched the doe hop away from them, toward the deep canyon. Then he waved at Malia to come next to him, closer to the outcrop of stone. Together, they peered around a cap of rock.

The deputy and the kidnapper walked into view, the deputy hiking a few feet farther away, to the edge of a depression in the plateau. Beyond them, a ridge of vertical cliff marked the start of the side canyon Relic had mentioned, the path to the bottom of the valley and the road out to the highway.

The deputy slid his pack off his back and rested his hands on his hips. The kidnapper moved to his left, staying behind him.

The deputy turned. "No sign of them here, either."

"I'm beginning to think we should turn back."

"The sheriff should be here by now. Maybe he's below us, working his way up, but I would have thought he'd have an airplane looking for us by now."

The kidnapper moved farther left, keeping his distance.

The deputy seemed to tense, then turned at the waist.

The kidnapper dropped to one knee, pulled a pistol from under his shirt, and just as the deputy stepped forward…

Blam!

She clapped her hands to her ears, the sound of the gun a cold, hard smack against her brain. She and Relic stared at each other, eyes wide, in a moment that stretched before them but then they turned to watch again.

The deputy rolled downward, into the low spot on the ground and out of sight. The kidnapper stood and took a cautious step forward, pistol raised to the sky.

Relic whispered, "Stay here. Hide."

"Where are you going?" Her voice hissed through her lips.

Relic grabbed his pack and tiptoed around the opposite side of the outcrop. Mae had reappeared behind the kidnapper, who seemed to have sensed her presence. He stopped and spun around, searching.

Mae hustled away.

The kidnapper turned away from the dip in the ground where the deputy had dropped and began to follow the deer past the outcrop where Malia and Relic were hiding. The man stopped and listened, his eyes searching from horizon to horizon until he finally relaxed. The pistol returned to its holster. The kidnapper moved farther away and sat on a rock, where he removed his daypack. He continued to watch the area where Mae had been. If only for a few moments, the deer had drawn his attention away from Malia and Relic.

Relic sneaked around the rocks and headed to the dip in the ground where the deputy had fallen, a direction opposite from where the kidnapper sat. Malia was even closer to the spot. She stepped carefully, keeping the outcrop between her and the kidnapper, moving away from it and toward where the deputy had disappeared. She followed Relic into the natural depression.

The deputy lay near the bottom, face down, his pack an arm's length away. Relic knelt by him and placed two fingers beneath his nose. Relic sat on his haunches and seemed to think for a moment.

He pulled a large knife from his belt and reached for the deputy's back.

What the hell was he doing?

CHAPTER 43

"Don't," she hissed.

Relic touched the knife to the deputy's spine and pulled his shirt away from his skin. He twisted the point of the blade into the fabric, spinning it to make a rough circle.

Then Relic cut his own arm above the wrist.

What? She took a step closer.

Relic squeezed blood from his wound and dripped it around the hole he'd made in the deputy's shirt. When he was done, Relic straightened the cloth, smoothing it against Dawson's skin.

From a distance, it looked like the deputy had been shot in the middle of his back.

Relic slid his knife into its sheath and glanced at her. "Hey," he waved her to the side. "Keep going that way," he pointed. "And get down behind those rocks."

There were rocks everywhere, but she understood. She hurried past Relic for several yards then lay behind a stone the size of a file cabinet. On her tippy toes, she could see just past the lip of the low spot where the deputy was.

Relic trotted to her left, up and out of the natural depression on the side opposite from where the kidnapper had shot the deputy.

"Hey!" The kidnapper ran back toward the edge of the small depression, pistol raised, aiming at Relic.

Blam!

Relic continued to run.

The kidnapper glanced below at the deputy's body and grinned. "Perfect shot," he said to himself. He turned and ran after Relic.

Relic was headed toward the canyon rim, his pack bouncing with each step.

She stepped down from her toes. Relic and the kidnapper were out of sight, past the ridge. He'd told her to hide but she had to see what was happening, so she hurried to the rise and plopped to the ground, her head just above the edge. Relic continued at a steady pace away from her and toward the cliff, the kidnapper about thirty yards behind. Relic trotted close to the rim, stopped, and faced the kidnapper.

He'd lured the man away from her.

The kidnapper quickly closed the gap, dropped to one knee like he had with the deputy, and pulled his pistol.

Blam! Blam!

Oh, shit.

Relic fell backwards, over the edge of the bluff, and disappeared.

CHAPTER 44

Malia's breath rasped through her windpipe like a clogged drain. She stared at the scene, transfixed.

The kidnapper walked to the rim of the cliff and peered over. He nodded and slid his pistol away. He stood there for several minutes, staring below, at a place she couldn't see, at a place where Relic had fallen, or been shot and fallen. He could be hurt. He could be dead.

The kidnapper put his hands on his hips and turned around slowly, a full circle, examining the area.

She lowered her head as his gaze swept toward her.

Oh my god.

It was time to get away from the kidnapper, out across the plateau, back to the cabinet-sized stone to hide. She crouched low to the ground and scurried across the small basin, back to the sheltering rock.

She dropped to the ground and wiggled to a spot

where she could once again see the deputy's body and watch for the kidnapper. Her throat was dry as the desert sand, her blood thick as pudding.

What was she going to do now?

The kidnapper came into view again, back atop the ridge above the basin. He walked along the high ground, watching the deputy's body for a while and scanning the landscape. He stopped and stood there, fists on his hips, and nodded to himself.

"Yes, indeed. Helluva shot."

He disappeared as quickly as a phantom, a mere glimpse of her own imagination. But he was real, she knew that. And deadly.

Silence coated the ground like a woolen blanket, the absence of sound heavy on her ears. She waited and waited, counting the seconds into minutes until she'd lost track. She raised her head a bit, searching, but the kidnapper remained out of sight. Gone for good, she hoped. She counted to a thousand again, just to be sure, then stood.

Thoughts plodded through her brain on muddy boots. The kidnapper had found them. Killed the deputy.

Shot at Relic.

Tears flowed down her cheeks like drops of rain.

She leaned against the low rock and peered across

the open ground. The deputy's pack still lay next to him. And that, she thought, could have water in it. But she'd have to go near the dead body.

She trudged her way across the sandy ground and around a patch of cacti, her eyes on her feet until she reached the man in uniform.

A low groan seemed to seep from the earth, and Malia leapt backward, ready to run.

The deputy was moving.

Relic had torn the man's shirt so the kidnapper would think he'd killed him. Relic must have known the man was alive.

Holy shit.

The deputy slid his right hand across the ground and rubbed his head, moaning loudly now.

She knelt next to his pack and searched for a bottle of water. "You're okay, you're okay."

The deputy pulled his elbows to his side and lifted carefully, a push-up of sorts. His head hung low, still touching the ground as he coughed, and coughed again.

He rolled to one side, sitting up as he went, and shook his head. His eyelids rose and he seemed to be searching for something until his gaze fell on Malia and the container of water in her hand.

"Here. Drink this."

He sat there for a moment, blinking, then tried to speak but croaked like a frog instead.

She realized that she should have taken the gun from him, but it all happened so fast and now it was too late. She removed the lid and handed the water bottle to him. He took it slowly, pressing it to his lips. After a first sip, he took a long drink, swallowing like his life depended on it.

When he was done, she took the bottle and lifted it to her own lips, taking a long, gut-filling drink.

"Who are you?" he asked.

"I'm Malia. Please," she felt the fear in her voice. "Don't hurt me." She was growing tired of saying those words.

"What? What happened?"

"I was kidnapped."

"Kidnapped?"

She nodded. "And who are you?"

"Deputy Dawson. And I'm not going to hurt you."

CHAPTER 45

Dawson ran a finger across his lips and wiped a bit of water from his mustache. His eyes were hazel with specks of gold and softened as he looked at her. "What happened?"

"That guy shot you." Her eyes scanned the deputy, searching for any injuries. "But I don't see any wounds."

"I caught him out of the corner of my eye, as he raised his gun, and as I turned, I tripped over the edge of that rim," he pointed. "And I guess I rolled down here, but I was out of it. Knocked out, I guess."

"Yes, completely out."

"What's going on?"

Malia sat cross-legged in the dust and explained the kidnapping and how Relic had pushed the trailer into the arroyo to rescue her.

"His name is Relic? Black hair in a ponytail?"

"Yes."

"Go on."

She told him about their hike across the plateau, Relic's plan to climb down a trail in the canyon nearby, a path that would take them to the downstream end of the dry creek. How they planned to go up to the dirt road, where she could hike out to the highway for help.

Dawson's face darkened with a thought. "Reed. He called himself Reed."

"I never knew their names or got a clear look at their faces, but I'm sure he's one of the kidnappers." She took another drink.

He reached for his pack and pulled out a small container of Tylenol. He popped two in his mouth and washed them down.

She held her open palm toward him, and he gave her two pills, too.

"There are three of them, claiming to be camping in an RV, claiming to be hunters." He felt his forehead and closed his eyes. "They fooled me, right at the moment we saw you run away with Relic. Reed volunteered to help me find you and find out what was going on. I never should have let him come along."

"He lied to you."

Dawson released a long sigh. "So, Reed is gone now?"

"Yeah, I think so."

"I remember hearing his gun go off. Or maybe I imagined it."

"Relic and I came to help you, but like you said, you were knocked out."

"And you got away from Reed?"

"Yeah, well…"

"Yes?" His voice was smooth and patient.

"Relic cut a hole in the back of your shirt. Then he cut himself and dripped blood on it so it would look like Reed had shot you in the back."

"What?" He reached behind his shoulder blades, feeling for the hole.

"Then we ran to that rock," she waved toward it. "He told me to hide there, and he ran the other way, out of this low spot. But I couldn't just sit there so I crawled to the rim up there and watched."

"What happened?"

Her throat closed for a moment, unable to speak. "Relic led the man away from me, toward the edge of the cliff, and the kidnapper shot at him. Relic went over the edge."

"Shit."

She nodded, tears raining from her eyes again. "I got back to the rock and that man—Reed—stood behind me and watched you for a while. I heard him say 'helluva shot' or something like that, then he went away. I waited to come to you, to see if your pack had any water and that's when I realized you were still alive."

They sat in companionable silence for some time, thinking.

Dawson clicked his tongue. "Well, that explains why we haven't seen the sheriff yet."

She looked at him.

"Reed's friends lied when they said they'd get Sheriff Leavitt to help us find you. Today's Sunday. That means no help until at least Monday, when I don't show up for work. Or more like Tuesday by the time they mobilize."

Malia was grateful to have Dawson on her side. And to know that someone would help them if they couldn't get to the highway on their own. She rested on the ground, gathering what strength she had left for whatever came next. Should they check on Relic? Maybe he was hurt. Maybe he was hiding.

"We need to go see about your friend Relic."

"I was just thinking the same thing." She reached into her pocket and pulled out a baggie. "Want some peanut M&M's first?"

Dawson's eyes bulged wide, and he nodded. After munching a handful each, they took another long drink of water. Dawson stood carefully, checking his arms and legs as if to make sure they were still attached. He straightened and slid the pack back onto his shoulders.

Malia took the lead, her first steps slow and stiff as she wound through the sagebrush and up to the lip of the basin. Once there, they both took some time to scan the horizon, making sure Reed was long gone.

Mae stepped from behind a knoll and watched them. Malia waved at the doe.

"What?" Dawson asked.

"That's Mae. She's a deer who hangs out with Relic sometimes."

"Really?"

"Yeah. I met her at our camp." She turned to Dawson. "She let me pet her and when we came to this area," she swept her arm in front of her, "Mae alerted us to you and Reed."

Dawson raised a brow, his question implicit.

"Mae noticed you first and we noticed her. So, we got down and hid as you guys went by us."

"Oh." He sounded impressed.

They walked toward the side canyon and the edge of the cliff close to where she'd last seen Relic. When they arrived, she hesitated.

"You look first," she said.

Dawson moved to the rim and peered over. He moved along the sharp edge, searching as he went, then stopped.

"I see clothing down there. A shirt, maybe."

"Oh." An image of Relic filled her mind, his tanned face, dark eyes, flimsy goatee. Hearty laugh. Tears swam across her eyes, blurring her vision.

"It's way down there, Malia. He could not have survived that fall."

She began to sob.

Dawson looked to the ground and shook his head. "No one could."

CHAPTER 46

Sheriff Leavitt rested his hands on the steering wheel and sighed. The search for Karl was beginning to feel like a waste of time. He removed the key and slid from the Jeep.

Across the street was Joel's Hardware Store, established 1957, a place you could get bolts, fishing poles, swimsuits, chicken feed, and just about anything else you could think of. Leavitt decided to check with Kelly, the manager, to see if he knew where Karl might have gone.

He checked both ways for traffic then crossed to the store. A bell rang when he opened the door, alerting staff to a customer's entry. A display of beef jerky greeted him, surrounded by bins with small plastic toys, tennis balls, and doggie treats. Chain saws were stacked along shelves to his right, barbeque grills along the aisle, the place nearly claustrophobic.

"Can I help you?" A cheery man with red cheeks,

graying hair, and a backroom smock approached the deputy.

"Kelly, how are you?"

"Good, Sheriff, what brings you here on this beautiful day?"

"I do need a new latch for my screen door, but…"

Kelly wiped his hands on his smock.

"I'll have to come back later for that."

"So…?"

"Our office has been following up on a missing persons report."

"Oh?"

"Have you seen or heard from our local handyman, Karl? Recently?"

"Heard from him?" His brows rose. "He just crossed the street, I think."

Leavitt straightened.

"Over there," Kelly pointed through the front window. "At least I'm pretty sure it was him."

Leavitt turned to look outside.

"Maybe headed to the Stockman's Bar."

"Do you recall what he's wearing?"

Kelly thought for a moment. "Blue plaid shirt, I think. Baseball cap."

The sheriff tipped his hat. "Thank you!" He hurried out the door and crossed the street again. Two buildings away stood the old bar, a local place that had more recently tried to attract travelers and tourists, the outside covered in rough-cut pine like an old western saloon.

A man with gray hair and whiskers, clad in a blue shirt, trotted across the road and into the bar.

"Hey!" Sheriff Leavitt yelled, but no one seemed to hear him. He shuffled forward, watching the entry to make sure the man did not come back outside. Maybe he'd found the elusive Karl, after all.

CHAPTER 47

Dawson walked farther along the rim, searching the ground. Malia gathered herself and followed. Focus on each step, she told herself. Each one until you reach your goal.

Shadows stretched to their left, out across the abyss, melting into the deep canyon below. She glanced about for any sign of Mae but could not see her. She craved her companionship.

Dawson pointed to the ground. "There's a trail here."

They crossed the rim, stepping down a row of stones onto a thin path that hugged the cliff. They were in the shadows now, below the horizon, winding from switchback to switchback down the steep incline.

Dawson turned toward her. "We should find a place to camp for the night. First place that looks flat enough."

From her vantage point, there didn't seem to be a flat spot anywhere on earth, the canyon edges ragged as torn paper, spires of rock, ledges of rock, chunks of rock fallen from the heights, rocks absolutely everywhere. They continued downward, her knees turning rapidly to rubber, her skin cooling in the breeze, and she lost all track of time.

Eventually, and to her surprise, the trail levelled out at one narrow spot, about mid-way to the canyon floor. A concave wall swelled above the site; a wave of Jurassic sandstone frozen in mid-curl.

"Here." Dawson scrambled a few feet under the roof of ancient beach.

She followed him up and nearly fell to the ground, exhausted. Her feet ached, her shoes were literally coming apart at the seams, and every ounce of her energy had evaporated.

Dawson set his pack on the ground and began gathering stones into a circle near her feet. He stumbled down the incline, skidding in one spot, and began gathering small pieces of wood that had fallen from the plateau above. She tried to rally herself. Seeing a small dead tree a few yards down the trail, she rolled to her feet and took small steps toward it. Once there, she broke branches off the dry trunk and dragged them back to the level spot below the stone shelter. Dawson had gathered more wood, too, and they soon had a stack nearby.

She sat on her haunches and stared out across the canyon to the wall opposite them, a smooth, high fortress. The rim glowed orange in the dying light, spiked like layered knives. Or even, she imagined, like the fiery scales of a medieval dragon.

Smoke stung her eyes, and a stack of sticks burst into flame. Firelight accentuated the ground around them, casting the canyon into deeper shadow. Dawson pulled a tin pot from his pack and set it near the fire. He poured water into the pot and set a plastic bag next to it.

"I don't know how old this is," he pointed at the bag. "But it's freeze dried, so it should be all right. Part of my emergency stuff."

She nodded.

After a while, he tapped half of the bag into the pot, spilling some on the ground, and stirred it with a spoon. He let it sit for a few minutes then handed it to Malia.

"Thank you." It smelled like spaghetti and hunger seemed to rise and swirl in her gut like lava. The food was warm and moist, and she shoveled it in with desperation she hadn't known was there.

Once done, Dawson took the pot and repeated the process for the other half of the freeze-dried meal. He moved to sit more comfortably but his own foot got in the way, and he banged onto the ground, nearly spilling his food.

"You okay?" she asked.

His cheeks flushed. "I'm a little awkward," he mumbled.

Dawson was strong and capable, but he seemed to think of himself as a stiff, nerdy type of guy. Clumsy sometimes and self-conscious about it. "Not half as awkward as me," she raised her brow.

Dawson gave her a thin smile and focused on his spaghetti, eating with gusto. She watched him for a moment, wondering what he was thinking and what he thought of himself. And wondering how she thought of herself, too; how she measured herself against others.

She looked up from their little fire. Night had swallowed the canyon whole.

Dawson shifted his legs. "This Relic character really tricked Reed into thinking I was dead?"

"Yeah."

"Astonishing."

"He risked his life for both of us. Who is he? I mean, who was he?"

"I've been chasing him around this country for a couple of years, thinking he was behind some bad stuff happening in these canyons, but now…I think I had it all wrong." He ran a finger across the dust.

"What else do you know about him?"

"Not much. He was a recluse. Rumored to have a couple illegal moonshine stills out here, but I never found them. But though I've encountered him a few times, my boss—the sheriff—and others, teased me that he was just a figment of my imagination. A ghost of the old pueblo ruins."

She shook her head, eyes clamped shut. "He was no ghost."

Dawson looked at her from under his brow. "Tell me about the kidnapping, if you can. Did you recognize who took you?"

"No, of course not. I mean, we went to a dance place, a fancy bar, and saw a couple of guys that gave me the creeps, you know? Seemed to be watching us."

"Us?"

"Me and my friend from college, Sheila."

"But isn't that what people do in those places? Check each other out?"

"Yeah, so it wasn't super creepy, just a little odd. Like they weren't interested in anyone but us."

"You think they're the ones who took you?"

"Maybe. Could have been. One was kind of big, the

other kind of skinny, but it happened so fast, I couldn't describe them any better than that. And then…"

"Yes?"

"One of them shoved a needle in my arm and I blacked out completely."

Dawson stopped moving, the spoon half-way to his mouth. "They drugged you?"

"I woke up in that old camper, scared out of my wits."

"I'm so sorry you went through all of that." He lowered his utensil.

"What I really don't understand, though…"

Dawson watched her.

"I don't know why they kidnapped me in the first place. I mean, why me?"

He canted his head and waited, a quiet urge for her to speculate.

"I was in a public place. But I guess I was a little off to the side. We were up in a balcony above the dance floor."

"So, they could drug you quickly without much notice."

"If they were quick. Which," she shook her head, "they were."

"And they could pretend you were drunk to get

you out of there."

"Yeah, but…did they pick me randomly?"

"Maybe."

"Or were they stalking me?" Her eyelid twitched.

"Maybe someone stalked you on your campus? You said you're a student, right? It wouldn't be hard to stalk someone going from class to class."

She thought about that.

"This friend of yours. Sheila. They could have taken her, too. Or instead, huh?" Dawson wiped the saucepan with a rag and stuffed it back into his pack.

"Right." Why hadn't they kidnapped Sheila instead? "No, that's *not* right, actually. Shiela was on the dance floor. I was in the balcony area by myself. I was alone. Isolated."

"Was there any special reason someone would kidnap you? Other than for money?"

"Like what?"

"I don't know, like revenge. Or politics."

She shook her head. She could think of no reason at all.

CHAPTER 48

Sheriff Leavitt pushed through the double door of the Stockman's Bar and into an entryway for stomping snow from winter boots and storing heavy coats. Beyond that hung a chest-high swinging door with wooden slats and a "Saloon" sign above it in 1800's style font.

He moved past the swinging door, to the side and away from the traffic pattern, and waited for his eyes to adjust to the darkened room. A thick walnut bar spread horizontally across the space; empty bar stools perched like crows along a fence. Country music filled the silence like a gentle breeze; there, but too remote to make out the words. Glass shelves with high-end liquor rose behind the bar, the wall behind them mirrored. To his right were signs for "Cowboy" and "Cowgirl" restrooms. To his left were round, wooden tables painted black. Four men sat at the one nearest the far wall; two men sat at the table nearest to Leavitt, their backs to him.

A sound like hammers on wood rumbled into the bar.

Leavitt turned to look.

A man's voice sang slow and slurred: "Whiskey and rum, whiskey and rum, thank you, sir, I'll drink till I'm numb."

The swinging doors kicked open and a donkey's head poked into the darkened room. Its hooves clomped again on the old pine floor, vibrations reaching Leavitt's boots, then it released a long, low bray that silenced all conversation in the bar.

Everyone turned to look.

The donkey took another step in, then another, and a man appeared on his back, the two of them sliding through the waist-high door and fully onto the open floor.

"Drinks for us all!" shouted the rider, cowboy hat in hand.

The swinging doors clacked against each other, slowing to a stop.

"Murphy!" The bartender said to the man. "You can't bring your donkey in here!"

"Whiskey and rum!" Murphy announced.

The bartender turned toward Leavitt. "Sheriff…"

Leavitt stepped closer to Murphy and his donkey. "Sir, you need to park your ride outside, like the rest of us."

Murphy's eyes grew wide, and he placed a hand on his hip. "Sheriff?"

"Yes, sir." Leavitt stepped even closer. "You're going to have to get your ass out of here."

Leavitt realized what he'd said, glanced down at his boots, and stifled a laugh.

The bartender joined in: "*Both* of your asses, Murphy! Out of here, now."

Murphy seemed confused for a moment, then pulled his chin to his chest, his feelings hurt.

"C'mon, Pinky." He patted the donkey's neck. "We know when we're not wanted." He straightened as best he could, indignant, and pulled the reins and kicked his donkey in the ribs. The animal grunted and turned a half-circle, hooves clomping again, and the pair of them stomped back through the swinging door and out of the bar.

The barman shook his head, a wide grin on his face. "There goes the original self-driving taxi."

"Oh?" Leavitt said.

"Designed by drunks for use by drunks. Old Pinky will get him home."

"If he doesn't fall off first," Leavitt added. "I'd better go see that he gets home all right. Or maybe he should stay in our cells 'till he sobers up."

The bartender nodded.

Leavitt chuckled, then remembered why he'd come into the saloon in the first place. The men on the far wall had begun to talk to each other again. The man in the blue plaid shirt and cap, at the nearest table, looked the sheriff right in the eye, his brow raised in amusement at the recent display.

He was not Karl.

CHAPTER 49

Stanovich signed out of the county computer and turned off the light on his desk. Sheriff Leavitt appeared in the doorway to the open room, scratching his back like a bear on a Cottonwood tree.

"Hi," Stanovich said.

The sheriff took a step forward. "Any news? Any new ideas on our missing man, Karl?"

Stanovich shook his head.

"I'm still a little surprised you don't know him. You grew up here."

"Yeah, Sheriff, but remember? My folks left town right after my senior year."

"Oh, yeah. Just a skinny teenager back then, huh?"

"Still am," Stanovich pointed to his thin frame.

"A teenager?" the sheriff teased.

Stanovich smiled. "Sometimes. But you know how

it is in high school. You care about your friends, the girls, of course. You hate your teachers and parents and homework. That's your whole world."

"True enough. No time for us adults with our grown-up problems."

"I just don't remember Karl. Or half the old-timers from here."

Sheriff Leavitt's face darkened. "I'm worried about the guy."

"Yeah."

"He's no spring chicken anymore. If he got himself somewhere in the outback and got hurt…"

Grace walked into the open area. "Excuse me, Sheriff, sorry to interrupt."

"Yes?"

"I need to leave early this week, if that's okay. My car is on the fritz and I'm catching rides."

"Sure," Leavitt said absentmindedly.

Stanovich gave her an understanding smile as she left the room. He turned to the sheriff. "I know what you said earlier about not re-checking places we've already checked."

The sheriff looked at him expectantly.

"But I could re-check the ruins and flats below Moonshine Mesa tomorrow, if you like. Work my way down to Star Chart Ruins. Dawson was sure that Karl might be out there, exploring."

"No, Dawson and I were just there." The sheriff backed into the door frame and scratched again.

"Yeah, you said there was nothing more to see there. Didn't he have a niece in Salt Lake?"

"I've tried calling but no dice. Left two voicemail messages." The sheriff stepped away from the door.

"Want us to go there? To Salt Lake."

"No, no. I'll call a friend of mine there tomorrow, a detective. He'll know who to put on the case."

Stanovich pursed his lips. "Sure."

The sheriff watched him for a moment, pondering something beneath the surface. Stanovich looked at his boss and gave him a quick smile.

The sheriff blinked; his thoughts diffused.

Stanovich wondered whether the sheriff really trusted him, whether he'd ever feel like he was part of the team here. He'd been an outsider in high school and despite his best hopes, he felt the same way now.

But then, maybe he hadn't tried hard enough to fit in. Or maybe it was never in the cards to begin with.

The sheriff turned and walked away. "See you in the morning."

"Yeah."

CHAPTER 50

Cooper lay back on the couch, belly full, beer in hand, contemplating all the ways he could spend two million dollars. Beaches. Women. Music. Parties. Boats. Fishing boats. Yachts. Cars—oh, cars! A red Porsche 718 Cayman coupe...

Boots clomped outside the RV. Cooper sat up quickly.

Reed opened the door and climbed inside, cheeks ruddy from the desert wind, shirt and pants coated in red dust.

"Hey, you're back," Cooper stated the obvious. "Let me get you a beer."

Reed plopped onto the couch, heaving a long, tired breath. He took two long drinks of the brew, set it down, and untied his hiking boots.

Cooper sat across from him at the small kitchen

table. "What happened?"

Reed released a sly grin.

Cooper clapped his hands together, smiling. If Reed was happy, Cooper was happy.

Reed leaned forward. "So, here's the scoop. The deputy is dead. Helluva shot if I say so myself."

Cooper took a swig.

"That guy with the ponytail—the one who rescued the girl—I got him, too. Shot him while he was at the edge of a cliff, the little shithead, and he went right over. I could see him down in the pile of rocks. Dead as a doornail." He sat back again and smiled from ear to ear.

"And the girl?" Cooper asked.

"Couldn't catch her. But she's good as dead out there with no food or water."

"Great work!" Cooper raised his bottle in the air, and they toasted to their success.

"How goes it on your end?" Reed asked.

"Well, Manning is worried out of his mind. I gave him the ransom payment instructions today and Hanna was around him when I called. Said he and his wife were waving their arms, pissed, upset. I figure they're having some problems getting the money together."

"That's not our concern."

"Right on that, my friend." Cooper leaned back.

"What if Manning wants some sort of proof that his daughter's alive?"

"We bluff. He's not likely to take a chance." He looked at the floor, contemplating something.

"What?"

"Well. On second thought, maybe he will take a chance. I mean, the dad could have jumped on it right away. On the first call, he hung up on me. Maybe it's because the girl is his stepdaughter, his wife's daughter from another marriage, I guess. Maybe he hasn't told his wife yet. Maybe paying the ransom for *her* daughter is making him nuts. Something is going on, there, I just can't figure it out."

"He's gotta come around, though."

"Right."

Reed looked around the RV. "Where's Teddy?"

"The chicken shit split. Got too nervous about the plan." Cooper took another drink, watching Reed's reaction.

"I told you that guy was dead weight."

"C'mon, man, he helped with the kidnapping."

Reed's face reddened. "He was worthless. I could've carried that girl on my own. Tell you the truth," Reed leaned forward, "it was a shit decision to bring that little shit into this gig."

"Hey…"

Reed leaned forward; his finger pointed at Cooper's chest. "It was a shit move."

Cooper's neck stiffened.

Reed sat back and crossed his arms, his point made.

Cooper looked away. "Yeah, well…"

"Good riddance, I say."

"Yeah, I guess so. He took the black pickup, but of course we still have the RV."

Reed thought about it. "And we have the deputy's truck."

Cooper nodded. "The little shit left me a note. Said he'd hid the truck battery because he didn't want us to follow him in it. Figured we're too slow to catch him in the RV."

"Who wants to catch him? Leaves more money for us." Reed raised his beer in the air. "Our exit plan still in place?"

"Absolutely. I'll call Hanna tomorrow for a final report. The ransom is by electronic transfer, so nothing awkward or risky for us. We'll take the RV to a spot near the highway, where a car will be waiting for us."

"Hey, I'm starving, man."

"Plenty of stew to heat up."

"Soon enough, it'll be filet mignon."

CHAPTER 51

MONDAY

The morning came cold and clear in their little snuggle under the cliffs. Sunlight burned the rim opposite from them, coral light sliding and thinning as it descended the sheer bluffs. The scent of last night's fire lingered in Malia's sinuses, spiced with sagebrush as the leaves warmed in the sun.

Her joints were so sore, she could barely move. After several tries, she sat up, winded even from that small effort. Dawson was as still as the dead and for a moment, she wondered. When he began to stir, she relaxed.

God she was thirsty. She found the water bottle and drank deeply.

Dawson turned and sat, his hair spiked like a man who'd been shocked, his mustache twisted away from his lips. "Mornin'."

She must look just as bad, she thought, combing

her fingers through her hair, brushing the dust from her blouse.

"How are you doing?" he asked.

"Okay. Stiff. Hungry."

Dawson stuffed his hat onto his head. "I've got some instant potatoes, but we need a fire and hot water for that."

She wrinkled her nose. "What is it with the potatoes?"

"What do you mean?"

"Relic had us eating that, too." The sound of his name made her stop. She let her eyes search down the narrow canyon and into the distance.

"Yeah." Dawson understood.

"Do you think we'll…find him? On our way down?"

He shook his head. "No. Not… I mean, no. We're too far in the middle of the canyon."

She released a sigh. "I have a few M&M's left."

"Where did you get those, by the way?"

"Relic."

"Oh."

She pulled the baggie from her pants and offered them to Dawson. They ate in silence, watching as daylight beamed higher in the sky, reaching farther into the dry creek bed like a hand into a glove.

They decided to skip the instant potatoes rather than gather more wood for a new fire. Malia chuckled at the idea of eating them cold. "I'm not quite that desperate. Yet."

Dawson stood. "Well, then, I guess we'd best get moving."

Malia slid her feet under her waist and tried to stand. Dawson reached for her and helped.

"Thanks." Using her feet, she pushed the stones in the fire ring apart, disbursing the gray ash across the little trail. Not as good a job as Relic had done, but not too bad, she thought. She noticed Dawson watching her.

Dawson started down the path, which quickly narrowed again. To their right, the bluff dropped hundreds of feet, her stomach feeling the pull. To their left, the sandstone wall rose to the top of the canyon. She stumbled over loose rocks, catching herself. She focused on where she planted her feet and, after a while, her muscles warmed a little. They were moving slowly but making steady progress. Already, she could no longer see their little campsite.

After several switchbacks, the trail suddenly ended in a small basin of sand, a place where water must pool when it rains. She leaned against the cliff. Dawson stopped farther down and looked at her.

She lifted a finger in the air, a signal for him to wait a moment.

Here, the canyon pulled into a narrow wedge, the sky but a ribbon of blue straight above her head. Though it was cool in the shade, she'd been sweating and now a chill ran down her shoulders.

"We're doing well," Dawson said from below her. "We're on the right path."

She didn't remember seeing a path at all, but of course there had to be one because they'd followed it to this spot. Did mountain sheep use this route? She gathered herself and pushed away from the sandstone wall. An outcrop of rock was piled to her left. She began to cross through them, following Dawson's boot prints.

A high-pitched hiss sounded from under one of the stones, the sound of a maraca but steady, without any rhythm. She bent down and peeked, though not too close.

A rope-thick rattlesnake, dark and coiled, stared into her face, its forked tongue flicking, its rattle so fast it was but a fuzzy smear in the air.

CHAPTER 52

Stanovich set a fresh coffee on his desk and turned on his computer. They'd still had no luck searching for Karl. He'd canvassed ranch owners and workers all around the place Karl had been doing odd jobs. He only had a couple of names left on his list——long-shots, at best. Stanovich didn't know Karl, but he had to admit that he was curious about the old guy. How many times have other people disappeared in this corner of the outback? He bet that every year, at least two or three, some of them never even reported. They just walked into the desert and turned to dust.

"Where the hell is Dawson?" Sheriff Leavitt's voice seemed to vibrate the windows.

Stanovich stood tall and waited.

The sheriff marched through the office door, boots clomping on the wooden floor. "Where is he?"

"I haven't seen him, boss. But it's only just twenty minutes after nine o'clock."

"Dawson's never late."

"Never?"

The sheriff stepped closer to Stanovich. "Dawson's a by-the-book, stiff-legged kind of guy." He rubbed under his nose. "A Dudley-Do-Right."

"Who?"

"The cartoon. Canadian Mountie Dudley-Do-Right. Goody two-shoes." The sheriff shook his head. "Never mind."

"I haven't seen or heard from him since before his time off." Stanovich watched the sheriff turn on his heel, full circle, a pirouette spun on frustration.

"I tried calling him earlier," the sheriff said. "Goes straight to voicemail. That's just not like Dawson and he's got a full duty schedule today."

"Yeah."

"That's all we need, damn it." He shook his head, his grizzled beard waving with the motion. "First Karl, now Dawson."

Stanovich thought his boss was overreacting but kept it to himself. Was Dawson really a stickler like that? Who cares about being a few minutes late? Besides, Dawson was a little quirky. He sure seemed to get away with more than most deputies would, in other counties. Chasing phantom moonshiners. Rechecking old leads on his time off. But the guy can't be a few minutes late to the office? Maybe rigid punctuality was part of that quirkiness? Stanovich still had a lot to learn about how Sheriff Leavitt ran his office.

"If we don't hear from him in the next twenty minutes, we go searching for him. I'll start at his house and make calls to friends as I go."

"I can go to Star Chart Ruins. Isn't that where Dawson last said he was going?"

The sheriff scratched under his neck. "Yeah, but I saw him there, looking for Karl."

"That's what I mean. That's the last place we saw him."

"He was okay when he was there."

"That was a couple of days ago."

"Yeah, I guess so. I would go but I've got a ten o'clock meeting with the county commissioners."

"So, then?" Stanovich asked.

"Go ahead. Question those hunters if they're still out there. But announce yourself first, clear and loud. You don't want them thinking you're an intruder and shooting your ass."

"Yes, sir."

"And don't linger. Dawson likes to hike in the Needles District and even a seasoned guy can get disoriented out there. Check quickly at Star Chart then hurry out to the Ranger Station at Needles. I'll start calling anyone I can think of."

Stanovich wrinkled his nose. "Dudley-Do-Right?"

Sheriff Leavitt's eyes narrowed. "If you knew him better, you'd understand."

"Right, boss." Stanovich stifled a grin.

CHAPTER 53

Malia stopped dead in her tracks, staring at the coiled snake, trying to fathom what she had encountered—a snake that could strike so fast she'd never even see it. Every muscle, every cell, every thought had jolted shut, clamped cold and rigid. What the hell should she do now?

Dawson appeared several feet away from her, pistol raised.

She'd stopped breathing.

Dawson sneaked a little closer.

The snake's tail continued to vibrate, a buzz, a blur, rattles warning her of deadly danger.

Dawson stopped.

The snake continued to shake its warning, its flat head steady, black eyes staring at her, forked tongue licking the air.

Blam!

The sound reverberated through the narrow canyon, crashing from one side to the other, echoes bouncing across the sandstone walls, overlapping as they rolled down the dry creek bed.

She couldn't move.

When she realized she'd closed her eyes, she opened them again. The bullet had eviscerated the snake, smearing it into the stones around it, red and yellow and black spattered across the ground.

She turned away.

Dawson holstered his gun. "Shit that was close."

She wobbled a few steps and plopped into the dust.

Dawson's hazel eyes bored into hers. "You okay?"

She nodded, her breath still ragged.

"We were lucky." He handed her their last bottle of water.

She took a sip. Dawson helped her stand up and they walked more slowly now, winding their way along the creek bed, Dawson ahead of her.

Her perspective seemed a little different now, images of the dirt and rocks and Dawson's boots especially clear but also flattened somehow, no longer three-dimensional. Her mind must be in some sort of adrenaline wind-down, she thought, affecting her vision. She kept walking, one foot in front of the other, and after a while the world seemed normal again.

Sheila had expressed a deep fear of snakes, but they hadn't bothered Malia. Until now.

She found a dead branch, something washed down from above, she guessed, and held it in front of her. When they came upon large rocks, she banged it against them like a blind man with a cane, testing the environment before stepping into it.

She was not going to be surprised by a rattlesnake ever again.

CHAPTER 54

The Mannings had cancelled their Sunday shindig. Something was wrong in the household, and Hanna was pretty sure what it was. They'd gotten a ransom demand and were in a twist about how to get the money.

Even though the party had been cancelled, there were tables to remove, food to give away or toss, dishes to collect and wash. She'd volunteered with her boss to help clean up, even though it was her day off. She wanted to be close to the action.

Hanna stacked glass party plates, placing a square of cardboard between each one. She set them carefully in two boxes and taped them shut. Mrs. Manning hustled through the room, ignoring her. Mr. Manning crossed the hall in front of her and entered his home office. Hanna knew that the dishes were stored in the garage. The office was down the same hallway.

She glanced around, assuring herself that she was alone in the large living area, and carried one of the boxes toward the office. The door was shut, but she could hear Mr. Manning's voice inside. She assumed he was on the phone.

"We need it *now*," his words slid under the door like smoke. The hall was empty, so she moved to the door frame.

The man seemed to be pacing across the floor inside. He grunted a word she could not decipher, clearly agitated. She leaned a little closer.

"Just what the hell do you think you're doing?" Mrs. Manning's voice shot through her nerves like an electrical charge, and she stumbled backward, into the wall, the box of plates nearly slipping from her hands.

"Oh!"

"What are you doing? Listening in?"

She'd been caught. There was no denying it. She cleared her throat and repositioned the box in her arms. "Sorry, ma'am, you scared me."

"Damn right I did. You're done here—what's your name?"

"Hanna, ma'am."

"You're fired. Go home. I'll call your boss and make it very clear to her."

Hanna's eyes moistened. "Please, ma'am, I really need this job…"

"Why were you listening to my husband just now?" Mrs. Manning crossed her arms, her head tilted.

Hanna thought quickly. "I heard a commotion. I'm sorry, ma'am, I…I just was drawn to it, you know? I heard voices and I guess they just pulled me in."

Mrs. Manning's eyes narrowed.

"I'm sorry. I'm sorry, I just, I mean, I got curious is all. Please, ma'am, I really need this job. It won't ever happen again."

Mrs. Manning shook her head, about to speak again.

"No, really. I'm working extra shifts—that's why I was here on Saturday—because my ex isn't paying child support. I have a two-year-old," now she was in full swing, making it up as she went. "I really, really need this job and I just got curious for a second, ma'am, just for a second, please don't complain to my boss or I'll be out of a job again."

Something in Mrs. Manning softened, her arms unfolding.

"I just heard something that sounded like trouble. I'm sorry." Hanna stepped back from Mrs. Manning, toward the garage door at the end of the hall. "I just need to put these away…"

Mrs. Manning waged a finger at her. "Don't let me ever catch you doing that again."

"No, ma'am." She turned away from her and hurried down the hall and into the garage.

She dared not get caught a second time.

CHAPTER 55

Cooper rubbed the beard under his chin and reached for the cell phone. He thought about what he needed to say and how he needed to say it, steeling his nerves for the call. Hanna had learned last Friday that the girl was not Manning's biological daughter, but his stepdaughter. Cooper hadn't revealed that he knew that—it might show the parents that Cooper had inside information. And the fact might explain Manning's reaction to the first ransom demand, but not his second. It was time to reach him again and put an end to the man's stupid delays. He placed the robotic voice modifier on his Adam's apple.

The phone rang on the other end, once, twice, then a hard click. "Who is this?"

Cooper spoke slowly into the phone. "You have six more hours to transfer the funds or your daughter dies."

Silence stretched out between them. Finally, Manning said, "I've told you to stop calling this number."

"Do you think this is some kind of *game*? We will shoot your girl dead in five hours and fifty—nine minutes."

"I thought you were going to let her die of hunger somewhere."

Cooper squeezed his free hand into a fist. "That was when I was being patient with you."

Thirty seconds ticked away, both men tense but quiet, waiting for the other to break.

"Screw you!" Manning shouted.

"Do you understand what I am saying?" Cooper raised his voice.

The stepfather hung up.

"What the hell?" Cooper stared at his phone like it had just insulted him. He dialed again, angry at the man's insolence.

This time, the call went to a voicemail recording. Cooper slammed the phone onto the kitchen table and cursed.

CHAPTER 56

They'd walked down the slot canyon for what felt like miles, the sandstone walls twisting like some prehistoric serpent, its tail whipping them left, right, over, back, never in a straight line. Malia had forgotten there was a sky above them, somewhere, blocked by rigid cliffs, a setting so radically different from the plateau above that the two hardly seemed capable of sharing the same planet.

Without warning, the canyon opened before them, a burst of sunlight, open sand, brush, grass, cacti, and sagebrush and beyond that, a single, shimmering cottonwood, its leaves crinkled and sun kissed.

They'd reached the dry creek bed, the one that would lead them upstream to the fancy RV and the kidnappers. A shiver ran down her neck.

Dawson stopped a few yards ahead of her and turned to wait.

The sun lay low on her right, warming the sands, casting shadows behind the sagebrush and rocks. They'd hiked nearly all day, and her legs ached like open sores. She knew if she stood there for long, she would not be able to start again.

"This is it, right?" she asked.

Dawson walked back toward her. "Yes. We should camp here tonight, along the cliff. My truck is up the arroyo, a couple of miles, maybe."

"Maybe?"

"I'm not sure. But we can go up the dry wash tomorrow and, hopefully, radio for help and get on out of here."

"Why not tonight?" As soon as she asked, she regretted it. Her feet, her legs, her lungs, all needed a long, luxurious bath. Certainly not another hike.

He beat the dust from his hat on his pants leg. "It'll be dark before we get there. I don't want to have to camp too close to the kidnappers. If we see them around, if we can't get out for any reason, we'll be stuck in the dark overnight. No fire."

"Okay." Thank god, she thought.

He pointed to an area to her right, tucked close to the bluff. The drainage curved gently the same direction until it met with the main arroyo, the one that led back to the kidnappers. She shuffled across the dry creek bed to the spot where Dawson suggested and beat her stick against a dresser-sized rock at the base of the cliff, warning any lingering snakes to get out of her way, she was coming in for a landing. She lowered herself into a sandy depression and leaned against the stone.

She closed her eyes for a moment, breathing deeply, and tried to relax her muscles. She pulled her right leg under her left, but her calf began to cramp. She straightened it quickly, pressing on her thigh with her hands until the pain subsided. She tried again more slowly, tucking each ankle under the other, cross—legged. Her throat felt lined with dry concrete, stiff and sore. Dawson had the water and he'd gone toward the arroyo and out of sight.

Slowly, her legs relaxed, and her thoughts drifted. Had the kidnappers called her parents? They must have by now. Was her mother going nuts? Yes, yes, she would just about lose her mind and it angered Malia. Could her parents even raise enough money to satisfy the thugs? What did they think she was worth? Her chest tightened, anguished at the thought of them tortured by a kidnapping demand they could ill afford to meet.

Dawson trudged toward her with a small load of driftwood. He dropped it nearby, came closer, and slid off his pack. "I'll get a fire set up."

She nodded. An orange glow hovered along the horizon, shadows now blending into other shadows. The sky became a melancholy shade of purple, a bruised transition into something new and sparkling.

"I've been thinking some more about the kidnapping." Dawson lowered himself to one knee. "And your friend who paid for your cover charge, your time at the fancy bar."

"Black Spider Lounge."

"Yeah. Do your folks have a lot of money?"

"Not really. I think of them as middle class."

"New cars every couple of years?"

"No. They've only ever bought used."

"Not a lot of cash in the bank?"

"Not that I've ever heard of. They're pretty careful with what they have. Why?"

"If your friend had a lot of money, and you don't, is it possible the kidnappers 'napped' the wrong girl?"

"That's crazy." She leaned forward, considering it. "They'd have to mix us up somehow."

"In the dark, in a noisy place…?"

Could Dawson be onto something? No, she thought, it seemed highly unlikely. Sheila was very different from Malia; she'd been thinking about that. How could anyone confuse Sheila with her?

Then again, she'd gotten her hair cut like Sheila's. And she'd been wearing her friend's shawl and holding her purse. And she'd been taking the same classes Sheila had been taking. Hanging out with the same friends, at the same bars, shopping at the same stores. If she was really being honest, maybe jealousy—just a little bit—had led her to conflate their identities.

She was suddenly quite unhappy with herself.

CHAPTER 57

Something was completely off about Mr. Manning's response to the ransom calls from Cooper. Hanna needed to find out more and she could only eavesdrop so often without getting caught. She needed to look at the man's office, in his records, letters, and desk.

Hanna moved her cleaning supplies into the hallway, keeping them close to the garage. Anyone looking for her would check near the garage first. That might help her gain more time in Mr. Manning's home office, about two dozen feet away.

She slipped on a pair of rubberized gloves and put a rag and a canister of cleaning spray into the front pocket on her smock.

She listened for a moment but heard no voices or shuffling feet. She puffed her chest and walked boldly to the office door, a maid proudly doing her job. She turned the knob slowly and stopped. Over her shoulder, she could see into part of the large living room and even a slice of the grand stairs leading to the second story. She could easily be noticed moving in or out of the office, so she waited, staring into those empty rooms, listening again.

Then she slid quickly into the man's office, closing the door behind her.

The walls on her left were lined with dark wood, mahogany, she thought, or something equally expensive. A desk made of similar, dense wood faced that wall. Six-foot windows rose on the far end of the room, exposing a lush lawn and hedges that arched down a gentle slope from the house. Framed diplomas and awards of various sorts hung on the wall along with a photo of men shaking hands, one with Mr. Manning holding a trophy of some kind, and one a graduation. Sheila's, she assumed. Opposite the tall windows was a clothes closet, one of its levered doors partway open.

She glanced around the room, at the four corners, and along a bookcase behind the desk, checking for cameras. The family had impressive security outside the house, but, luckily, did not seem to have them inside.

Hanna hurried to the desk and began reading papers stacked on an end and several others on top of a flat ink blotter. The computer was off. She didn't know Mr. Manning's password, so she figured she couldn't get inside it.

Her fingers touched letters from Mr. Manning's mining company, reports on production, nothing helpful to her. She opened the left drawer and rifled through the files there. What was she hoping to find? She had no serious theory about Manning's behavior. Had he even told his wife about Cooper's calls? Despite the obvious wealth, was he having financial problems? Was five million too much to ask to ransom his daughter? Well, stepdaughter, but still…

It made no sense to her.

None of the files looked interesting, except the last one, marked "Personal." She lifted it from the drawer and placed it on the desk.

A muffled noise made her stop.

Someone in the living room, she guessed. She opened the folder and searched through the pages. One showed a "Net Loss Statement," financial numbers of some sort, a setback in a company she assumed that Manning owned. Maybe that was it. A serious debt. A cash flow problem. Maybe he needed more time to mortgage this mansion. Or maybe it was already mortgaged.

She continued turning pages, scanning as she

went. As soon as she was finished here, she resolved to call Cooper with this new information about the man's finances. Or maybe it was just a new theory. Either way, Cooper needed to know.

A tap sounded just outside the office door.

Her throat constricted. She shoved the papers into the file and slipped it in the drawer. Gently, she pushed the drawer back into place.

The door handle began to turn, then stopped.

The motion released a primal reaction—flee or hide, flee or hide, the question flashed through her brain like lights on an ambulance. She couldn't get caught by the wife again, not a second time. That would be the end of her job, for sure. And probably worse.

The doorknob did not move again.

As quietly as she could, she hurried to the closet opposite the side of the desk. She spun inside and pulled the partially open door behind her. She dared not close it all the way for the sound it might make. Men's suit jackets hung on the rack, and she backed slowly into them, pulling their sleeves in front of her.

"Darling?" Manning's wife stepped inside his office. "Are you in here?"

Hanna could hear her march to the front of his desk and stop.

"I could have sworn…" she mumbled. Footsteps came right up to the closet door and the woman shoved it closed with a snap and a crash and a harsh metal clack.

Hanna's heart nearly stopped, her breathing ragged, her mind in a soup of panic.

Then his wife walked away, closing the office door behind her.

CHAPTER 58

The light under her eyelids grew brighter and brighter, forcing her slowly awake. Malia rolled onto her back and stared at the pale morning sky. She sat forward, crossing her legs beneath her. Dawson was maybe fifty yards away, walking along the other side of the drainage that led from the narrow canyon they'd descended last evening. She rubbed her eyes then reached for the water bottle and took a long drink.

Dawson waved at her. She nodded in reply.

Her muscles had stiffened over night, but she forced herself to stand and stretch. Dawson moved farther away, searching the ground as he went. What was he looking for over there?

A low rumble seemed to vibrate from her toes into her knees, a distant engine maybe. Clouds had moved into view just above the canyon rim, dark over the far horizon.

They were almost to the kidnapper's RV, almost to the road and out of danger. Her skin tingled with the thought of coming closer to the thugs who'd taken her, but thoughts of steaming coffee and pancakes and juice and a hot shower outweighed the risk. Besides, Dawson said they could cut across the canyon to intercept the dirt road; avoid the RV and slip away unnoticed. God, she hoped he was right.

Another resonance, low and grumbling, rose into her spine. Dawson looked up quickly, noticing something, too.

She walked closer to the arroyo and toward the slot canyon, where the sensation seemed to emanate. She stood on the edge of the dry bank and listened.

The mouth of the canyon seemed to wheeze like a living beast, exhaling a burst of cool air and an unusual roar, deep and powerful. Dawson suddenly ran towards her, waving his arms, shouting something she could not hear.

The sound rose like a turbine engine, overwhelming all other noise, and she stiffened. Suddenly, a surge of copper-colored fluid, loaded with silt and sand, poured from the narrow canyon. Her feet slipped off the edge of the bank, sliding into the creek bed and toward the churning water.

She twisted toward the bank and fell into it, clawing the rocky side to stop her descent but the slope was too steep. Her feet soon found the icy water and the cold swirled around her ankles, then her calves, as she continued to scramble against the pull.

The water lifted quickly, tugging her deeper into the flow and she soon splashed into it, waist-high, spinning away from the high bank and down the arroyo with the rising flood, no way to stop.

Dry for months, maybe years, the drainage was suddenly a full-throated, roaring creek. She knew that a mere two feet of water would carry away a car and each time she tried to plant her feet underneath her, the flow tossed her backwards.

In moments, she'd travelled thirty yards downstream.

The creek pushed toward a sharp bend and a downed cottonwood, swirling her into the bank and against the rough bark, pinning her against it. She found the stub of a branch above her and grabbed it as the water rose to her chest, her neck. She pulled herself as high as she could, a one-handed chin-up, and clawed her other hand into the dead tree bark. The flood seemed to level for a moment, then crept higher up her neck, to her chin, to her nose and she took a deep breath of air, fighting to stay above the icy water, but it was too much, too fast, and she was underneath the swirling flow.

251

CHAPTER 59

How long could she hold her breath? Malia tried to lift herself higher, pulling harder, to no avail. Slivers of light flashed across her vision, and she fought the urge to breathe. She began counting the seconds, one, two, three…twelve…fifteen, when something shifted, the water dropping down below her eyelids. She blinked open, stretched her neck and head back, and swallowed the air in sucking gasps.

The water continued to drop, down below her neck, her chest, down to her waist. She hugged the dead tree, breathing hard, watching the frothing brown liquid twist around her and onward, downstream.

The growl of churning water softened as the level continued to fall, to her knees, her calves, and finally to her ankles. Everywhere, the flood dropped like a bathtub with its plug pulled. She searched for Dawson, but he was nowhere to be found. She crawled higher along the tree and rolled into the dust along the bank, out of the arroyo. Blue sky stared down at her face, a hot autumn breath drying her skin.

She sat up, propped on her arms, and locked her elbows. Dawson waded across the fading flood, lifting his feet out of the flow in exaggerated steps. He reached the other side and climbed the bank on hands and knees. She pulled a string of wet hair from her face.

"Malia! Are you okay?"

"Now I am, yes." She leaned forward, hands on her knees.

Dawson sat across for her. "Holy crap that was fast."

"Fast?"

"Flash floods can happen fast, but that was…crazy."

She could see pewter-colored clouds above the canyon rim, the source of a rainstorm, and of course, the flood.

"I slid down the bank," she pointed. "I was swept downstream, 'till I hit that dead tree."

"A strainer."

"A what?"

"Sometimes called a strainer, they're really dangerous. You can get tangled up in them, or held under them by the water, and drown."

She closed her eyes. "I nearly did."

He touched her ankle with his hand, hazel eyes speckled with brown, green, and gold, and she realized how much she liked them. She pulled her eyes toward the ground and took another deep breath.

"I'm glad you're okay."

"Yeah. Me, too." She squeezed water from her hair. "Help me up?"

Dawson lifted her under her armpit.

"Do you mind looking away for a minute?" she asked.

"Uh, sure." He turned away.

She unbuttoned her blouse and peeled the wet fabric from her skin. She wrung the water from the cloth, shook it out, and put it back on, the polyester cold against her back. She slid out of her shoes, water squirting from the seams, and dropped her pants to the ground. Balancing one leg at a time, she removed and wrung her slacks out as well as she could, then slipped them back on.

"I'm done," she said.

Dawson turned back towards her.

She lifted each shoe, pouring water into the dust. "What were you looking for, earlier?"

"I saw an old pickup farther up the main arroyo. I'm wondering if it could belong to one of the kidnappers."

"Oh." She slid her feet into her shoes and watched as the seams slid open. They weren't going to last much longer.

"Or maybe not. We're a fair distance from their RV. I don't know why someone would have left it where it is unless maybe it broke down out here."

She stepped closer to the edge of the bank. The roaring flood had melted away, seeping into the dry sands, spreading across the creek bed, flowing around a bend and out of sight. She stared at the wet arroyo.

"See how this bed comes out of that narrow canyon? The one we hiked down yesterday?" He pointed left.

"Yeah?"

"That drainage is below the main one, which is over there." He pointed straight ahead. "So, the flash flood came down our little canyon, this way, past where we are now."

"Right. And?"

"Well, the main arroyo, the one that will lead us to the road and out of Slickrock Canyon, is upstream of the canyon that just flooded. So, we cross back over, then the rest of the way will still be dry."

"I see. Clear going from here on?"

His lips rose in an uneven smile. "Sure as hell hope so."

CHAPTER 60

Reed leaned his knuckles on the side of the doorway. He could feel the frustration rising in his chest. "We're already one day later than we'd planned."

"Can't be helped. Hanna just called. She says she thinks Manning is having trouble getting cash together for the ransom." Cooper sat back on the couch.

"First, we think the man's resisting because the girl is his stepdaughter. Now he's having trouble raising the cash?"

"It's entirely reasonable. Both things are true, and both are slowing down Manning's reactions."

"But he's not answering your calls anymore! Something else is wrong." Reed's words settled in the air. "Was that kidnapping you did a couple of years ago this hard? Hadn't the wife paid up right away?"

"Yeah…"

"I'm telling you, Cooper, we can't wait another day to get out of here."

Cooper raised his hands, a gesture of surrender. "I'm worried about it too, all right? I'll call Hanna at the end of the day and get another update."

"I'll see if I can find the battery that Teddy hid out there. And make sure we can start the deputy's vehicle. It'll be faster if we can leave this canyon in a pickup truck." Reed waved at the RV, opened the door, and stomped outside.

Reed knew that Cooper had put a whole plan together last year. The surveillance of the Manning residence, the job placement for Hanna as their "inside" source, the crypto account the ransom would be paid into. But now Cooper was hanging onto hope too long, listening to his girlfriend Hanna when he should be dropping this whole thing and getting them out clean. Maybe Cooper was getting too greedy. Or maybe it was Hanna.

They needed to get the hell out today.

Reed kicked the dust at his feet and looked out over the dirt road. Behind him, the arroyo led into the canyon where he and Dawson had first followed the girl and the ponytail man. He smiled to himself. At least those three problems had been solved.

He walked toward the Deputy's truck, looking for

places where Teddy might have placed the battery. He got to the vehicle and opened the door. He'd heard that rural law enforcement left spare keys in their vehicles in case the officer driving it got into trouble or reinforcements needed to move the vehicle. He lowered the visors, searched in the glove compartment, felt between the seats. Nothing.

Maybe a key was in one of those magnetic boxes, stuck under the front bumper. He knelt to the ground and searched, fingers running along the inside edges of any place that might work. Still, no luck.

He moved back to the cab and stared at it for a moment. A radio set had been bolted on top of the dash, the coiled microphone wire dangling toward the gear shift. Mats covered the floor, clods of dried mud, sand, and dirt filling the rubberized pattern. He lifted the corner closest to the door.

There it was. A spare fob tucked between the rubber and the carpet. He slid it into his pocket.

He popped the lock and moved to the front grille. He raised the hood and stared at the empty battery holder.

Damn it, Teddy, he thought. Always the bullshit with Teddy. Cooper said the note from Teddy wasn't very clear about where he'd put the battery. But a battery is heavy, and Teddy would not have gone far to hide it.

He'd look around for it but if he didn't find it, maybe he could put the RV battery into the pickup. They could travel a lot faster than in the RV and maybe even listen to the police radio at the same time. Monitoring the sheriff's office could turn out to be very helpful.

Reed looked at the Star Chart Ruins, at a single storage "granary" on the western edge of the site. Though it looked old, he knew it was brand new. And he knew it hid an old man inside.

He walked toward the ruins, then back toward the arroyo, in a search pattern for the missing battery.

CHAPTER 61

Malia and Dawson walked back to their little camp, where his pack rested against a small boxelder tree. Her shoes squished with flood water, but her blouse was quickly drying in the sun.

They'd eaten some sort of lukewarm instant mush last night. They'd also eaten the last of the peanut M&M's. A small pool on the other side of the arroyo had given them plenty to drink. Dawson had used a filter to squeeze out all the worst of the germs: Giardia, Salmonella, E. coli, Cryptosporidium. They'd saved two large pieces of BBQ beef jerky for breakfast, the final bits of their food.

Malia sat on the ground, dust adhering to her wet pants. She ate the jerky slowly, savoring the taste; there was nothing like hunger to enhance the joy of a sweet, salty meal.

Dawson tossed the rocks they'd used as a fire ring into the empty creek bed. Sunlight filtered through the leaves, a hint of autumn in the cool breeze.

"Ready?" he asked.

"No. But…" she stood slowly, using the cliff wall to help straighten her legs.

"Today, we keep a real close watch. If I'm right, we'll get to my pickup in two miles, maybe less. As long as you stay out of any more floods." He glanced at her under his brow, lips in a grin.

"Ha, ha," she said, returning his smile.

They left their little shelter by the bluff and moved across open ground. They crossed the wet arroyo to the larger drainage and began a slow ascent as it rose toward the main canyon where she'd been held captive four days ago.

"There," Dawson pointed. "That abandoned pickup truck."

A faded blue Ford sat about fifty yards away.

"The kidnappers'?"

"I thought so at first but now I doubt it. It's too far from their RV to be of much use to them."

"Like you said, maybe it broke down out here and the owner just left it."

"Maybe."

They continued walking for nearly a half mile before they stopped for a short break. A giant cottonwood, alone in the sand, cast its morning shadow across the dry creek bed. The ground was flat and hard in the center, the easiest walking as the arroyo twisted left, right, then straight for a while. An unwelcome smell reached her sinuses. Dawson stopped ahead of her and held his nose for a moment.

"What is it?" she asked.

He pointed. "Over there."

They walked another thirty yards or so and around a bend. There on the ground lay a dead buck, its head at an unnatural twist, small antlers dug into the sand, tongue blackened and hanging in the dirt. Flies buzzed around its marble-shaped eyes.

"Oh," she turned away, images of Mae filling her mind.

"He's been shot." Dawson moved closer to examine the deer.

"Shot?"

"Yeah." He pointed to a spot of blood, a hole in its hide beneath the ribs. "It's not deer season yet."

She thought of Mae again, her soft black nose, bulging eyes, hot breath. Was the buck a relative of hers? A suitor? Her face flushed with anger.

"It's one thing to kill for meat to feed your family," Dawson turned toward her. "But killing an animal just for the hell of it…" he shook his head.

"It's a crime," she agreed.

"Morally, yes, and legally, too. It's poaching." Dawson came closer to her. "And it's a fresh kill. Those so-called hunters, no doubt."

"My kidnappers." The word just popped out of her mouth but her own use of the word "my" felt strange. "Her" kidnappers, she thought. An ownership. Ownership of what had happened to her.

"It shows they're in the area. And…" he hesitated. "Of course, they have a rifle."

They looked at each other for a moment and Malia nodded.

"Didn't you say we could cut across the canyon to the dirt road? Avoid the kidnappers that way?" she asked.

"Yeah, but I think we can go farther up the creek bed before we cut across. Go too early, and we'll be hiking over rough ground for a lot longer than we have to."

Great, she thought. Their choice was either a lot more hiking or a lot less safety. She hardly had the energy to decide. But at least the deputy had a gun.

"Okay."

Dawson led the way farther up the arroyo, more

slowly now, stopping to listen from time to time. Malia's blouse had dried completely in the desert air, her pants dry everywhere except at her waist. Eventually, they came to several young cottonwoods and climbed to the top of the bank to look around. They'd arrived at one end of the Star Chart Ruins. She could see a stone structure of some sort next to cliffs that curved ahead of them.

"We're closer to the kidnappers than I thought. Look," Dawson whispered. "My truck."

She searched the open ground to their right and saw it; a tan truck with a sheriff's star on the side door.

A burst of hope surged through her. "Can we just get to your truck and drive away?"

"But why is the hood up?" Dawson asked.

CHAPTER 62

Dawson and Malia crept quietly along the top left side of the arroyo, a few feet from the bottom of the dry creek bed. They approached the deputy's pickup truck from the front, searching for anyone who might be nearby.

They crossed a flat surface that was empty of grass and brush. The road leading out of the canyon lay on their right, just past the truck. Dawson crouched low and approached the fender, Malia close behind him.

He lifted himself to the edge of the engine compartment. The raised hood blocked their view of the RV, which was parked about fifty yards farther up the road.

Malia glanced back the way they'd come, wishing they had the cottonwoods to hide behind. They were exposed out here in the open, with only the truck itself as a shield if any of the kidnappers came around.

Dawson's words whistled through his teeth: "Damn

it. They took the battery out."

She peered under the hood.

He whispered, "There's no way to drive it out of here and no power for the radio, either. We can't call for help from here."

"Now what?" she asked.

His lips clamped tight under his mustache as he thought for a moment. "We're closer now than if we had cut across earlier, but it's still gonna be a long hike out to the highway. Several miles."

Her shoulders collapsed, lungs emptied, and she leaned her weight on the side of the truck. "Don't tell me that. I'll try, but I don't know if I can go for *miles*."

"I can go. You can stay hidden, back by the trees," he pointed behind them.

"By myself?" She heard the desperation in her voice and regretted it.

Something sounded to their left, beyond the truck.

They looked at each other. Malia lowered herself to a squat while Dawson looked carefully past the hood of the truck.

"See anything?" she murmured. Maybe it was Mae, or another doe, wandering the canyon, searching for the dead buck. But that was probably wishful thinking.

Dawson slid quickly to the ground, a single word

expelled with a burst of air: "Shit."

Now she knew it was no deer.

Footsteps came closer to the truck, grass rustling against someone's pants. Malia dropped to her hands and knees and peered under the body of the truck.

Hiking boots.

The man stopped. Malia held her breath.

The boots began moving again, toward them, toward the truck.

Dawson motioned for her to crawl to the rear bumper. She moved slowly, watching the man's legs as she crept. Dawson came up behind her, both of them now at the rear of the pickup.

The man stopped again.

They waited a minute that felt like an hour. The man walked away from them this time. He seemed to be searching for something.

She stuck her head past the bumper for a better look.

It was the kidnapper, the one who'd chased her and Relic up the other canyon and across the plateau. The one who'd shot at Dawson. The one who'd killed Relic.

The man turned again, scanning the ground, this time coming directly at the pickup truck.

Dawson unsnapped his holster and slid his pistol out.

CHAPTER 63

Hanna set her mop aside and lifted the cell phone from her pocket.

Cooper's voice was tense, urgent. "Can you talk?"

She was in the hallway that led from the garage, past Manning's home office, into the huge living and entertaining area. Mr. Manning had left. She overheard his wife say something about the FBI. She hadn't overheard or learned anything else about his efforts to gather money for the ransom, and it had her worried. The wife had gone upstairs to take a phone call. Hanna's boss was in another part of the house, preparing it for guests.

"I can talk for a minute, but not too long," she breathed into the phone. "I heard them say to call the FBI but I don't know if they did that or not."

"Damn it. What's wrong with those people? Don't they want to see their daughter alive again?"

"Hey, no one gets hurt in this deal," she hissed.

"Of course not, babe, we just have to make them believe it. That's all I meant. Those parents should be protecting their daughter, not calling the FBI."

"What do we do?"

"Let me think."

She lifted the mop into the bucket. "Did you make another ransom demand?"

"Yeah. Manning ignored it; even let it go to voicemail."

"He's worried about something."

"Yeah, but what? Is it possible he gave up on getting the cash?"

Hanna moved down the hall toward the living room. "That can't be it. You should see this place, Cooper. It's…huge and filled with crystal glasses and fancy paintings and sculptures, and it's got to be worth millions and millions."

"I'm gonna try one more time, as soon as we hang up."

"Mr. Manning's not here, so I can't tell you how he is acting or what he says after the call."

"Maybe it's time to call the wife. The girls not adopted, is she? Or maybe the mother is out of the picture, not living with Manning and his wife."

"No, I think the wife must be the mother; I think Manning is the stepdad. But I couldn't find out for absolute sure."

"No?"

"I'm the cleaning lady, Cooper. I couldn't just march up to her and ask that, now, could I?"

"No need to get heated, babe."

Her face flushed. Nothing got her angrier than Cooper telling her not to get angry.

Someone came stomping down the steps on the opposite side of the large room. "Hang on," Hanna slid her phone into her pocket.

The front door opened; someone had come home. Maybe Mr. Manning. She lifted a spray bottle and rag from her supply cart and moved with purpose across the floor, determined to dust the handrail on the staircase, a place where she could hear and see what was happening.

The door slammed shut and the voice of a young woman squealed with joy. "Mom!"

Hanna came to the edge of the large room and was about to reach for the railing when Mrs. Manning rushed down the stairs.

"Sheila! You're home early!" Mrs. Manning spread her arms and the two hugged tightly in the foyer.

Hanna slid back into the living room, turned, and

scurried back to the hallway. "Cooper!" she whispered.

"What's going on?"

"It's Sheila. She's *here!*"

"What the hell?"

"It's Sheila, the girl you kidnapped. She's home."

"That *can't* be. She's dead or lost up on the plateau out here. She can't possibly be home."

"Well, she *is.*"

"What the hell?"

"Did you guys even kidnap the right damned girl?"

CHAPTER 64

Hanna stepped farther into the hallway and leaned against the door to the garage.

Cooper had really messed it up this time. Why does she keep falling for screw ups with giant plans for success? She was trying to win the lottery over and again with the same man, the same impossible odds. Cooper's plan seemed foolproof but somehow, he or his crew had screwed it up.

What could she do now? She thought of her sister in Bozeman. Could she get there without being arrested? Could she hide in the mountains of Montana?

Sheila was not the girl who'd been kidnapped, which probably meant Mr. Manning had called the FBI as soon as he'd gotten the ransom call and realized his daughter was all right. The feds might be investigating already. Which meant that, sooner or later, they'd be interviewing everyone in the household, including the cleaning people.

Her chest tightened and her knees seemed to melt. She meant to be safe, just an observer, the 007 spy, but now they would question her, pressure her, confiscate her phone, oh, shit, she had all those calls to Cooper. She turned toward the garage door and opened it.

"Hey!" Mrs. Manning's voice seemed to bang in her ears.

Hanna moved quickly, stepping into the garage and slamming the door behind her. She ran past a black BMW, weaving between it and a Cadillac Escalade, her fingers sliding over the slick hood. A wide Hummer was next in line, taking up two parking spots. Beyond that were two four-wheelers, parked sideways along the wall.

The door behind her squeaked on its hinges.

She headed for the garage door opener and pushed the plastic button, once, twice, and again. The motor began to grind, the large door clunking as it began its ascent.

Mrs. Manning's voice rose an octave. "What are you doing? Come back to the house!"

The door rolled slowly higher.

"Hey!"

Hanna knelt on the ground.

Mrs. Manning clomped across the concrete floor

alongside the BMW.

The door rose two more inches.

Hanna looked up across the rear of both cars. Mrs. Manning stood at the opposite end, hands on her hips, then began a quick march toward Hanna.

The door clunked again, stuck for a moment, then rumbled past it. Hanna rolled to the ground and under the door, barely squeezing through.

She stood and ran as fast as her legs could carry her, across the concrete pathway, across the fertilized lawn, to the trees that bordered the property. She grabbed the trunk of a small Maple and spun to look behind her.

"Hanna!" The garage was fully open now, both cars exposed, Mrs. Manning standing on the driveway.

Hanna turned and ran through the brush, deeper into the trees. What had she done? In a moment of panic, she'd made it all worse, much worse. She'd made herself look guilty as hell and now she'd have to flee from the FBI.

She'd bought her last lottery ticket with her last dollar and now it looked like she'd lost again.

CHAPTER 65

Cooper turned off the satellite phone and sat by the kitchen table, lips slack, arms loose, eyes staring into the distance.

Teddy and Reed had taken the wrong girl. How the hell did that happen?

Cooper stood and smashed his fists on the table, again and again, swearing, spinning in a circle, smashing the table in another round of flaming anger, his lungs heaving like a boxer in battle.

After four minutes of smacking, cursing, kicking, fuming, more banging on the table, more smacking, cursing and kicking, he finally collapsed onto the couch.

Reed and Teddy had clear instructions, clear directions. Hanna had seen Sheila leave the house at about six in the evening. The girl wore a dark blouse with a white shawl. Medium height. Shoulder length brown hair. She showed up at the fancy nightclub with a friend. Teddy and Reed followed her in and watched for a while, waiting for the right moment.

How could they have taken the wrong girl?

As soon as he asked himself the question, he knew the answer: they'd taken Shiela's friend. In the dark bar, strobe lights on a dance floor, they'd mistaken one for the other.

Sheila's stepfather failed to respond to the ransom demand then stopped taking his calls all together. Then, as Hanna reported, the man may have called the FBI. His ransom demands had rattled Sheila's parents, but they must have thought it was a crank call. Sheila had been just fine all along, and they must have known it. The first thing they would have done was call their daughter to check on her. "No," she'd have said. "Right here. Not kidnapped. All fine."

He pounded on the table again.

Cooper had been calling the wrong set of parents. Five million dollars down the drain. Never in the drain to begin with. Never even in the same house as the drain, *damn it*.

Reed was out looking for the battery that Teddy hid and to see if he could hotwire the deputy's truck.

They had to get the hell out of there.

CHAPTER 66

Dawson turned toward the front of the truck; his gun raised at the ready.

"Don't you dare make a move." Reed's voice chilled her bones. They turned to see him a few feet away, at the rear end of the truck, pistol aimed at Malia's head.

Dawson slid his gun back into its holster. He held his hands away from his utility belt, fingers splayed.

"Can't say I'm happy to see *you two here*." Reed motioned for them to stand up. "I killed you," he looked at Dawson.

"Yeah, I thought so, too."

He nodded at Malia "And I left you for the vultures."

They raised their hands higher as they stood.

Shit.

So close, she thought. So close. Her knees began to

buckle but she locked them in place and leaned against the side of the truck.

Reed's eyes were mere slits below his brow. "Good thing Teddy lifted that battery after all."

"You won't get away with this," Dawson announced with a bit too much bravado. "The sheriff will be on his way by now."

Reed grinned. "Not exactly clairvoyant, are you?"

"What?"

"Put your gun on the ground," Reed said.

Dawson removed it slowly from the holster and obeyed.

"Now, put your keys to the truck on the roof."

Dawson did as he was told.

"Start walking," Reed pointed toward the naked cliffs.

Dawson shuffled ahead of her, Reed behind them. The man tucked Dawsons' sidearm into his belt. He was going to kill them, she thought, right here in the outback, where the vultures and coyotes would chew on their bones. The realization alchemized into a brick of clay in the center of her gut.

Dawson stumbled and caught himself. They continued across open ground toward a closet-sized ruin tucked under a ledge. The rocks that formed its walls were crooked and rough, not like the carefully chiseled stones of the pueblo ruins a couple of yards away.

They came to a pile of broken sandstone. "Stop here. Start stacking," Reed commanded.

Dawson glanced from the ruin to the loose stones and back again. "What?"

"*Oh.*" Malia suddenly understood.

Dawson's eyes went wide, like he'd realized something, too. His chin fell to his chest, and he stepped to the "ruin" and touched the wall. "This is Karl in here, isn't it?"

"Karl?" she asked.

Dawson nodded. "Missing for several days now. Nice old guy. Likes to check out the pueblo ruins and makes some pretty cool sketches of them. I bet that was his truck we found in the arroyo."

Reed waved the pistol back and forth a bit. "Yeah, yeah, old guy found us out here getting set up, before we were ready. Nosy bastard, too." His chuckle held a sharp, mean edge.

Dawson's face flushed tomato-red. "You killed him!"

Malia thought Dawson's head would burst.

"Start stacking another ruin, 'cause you're next." Reed lowered to one knee, the position he'd used to fire on them up on the plateau. He aimed first at Dawson, then moved the barrel of the gun toward Malia, his smile like a crack in a tombstone.

CHAPTER 67

Dawson's arms fell loose at his sides, his cheeks suddenly void of color, his eyes flat as coins. Malia's knees released her to the ground, exhaustion, defeat, and the gravity of a small planet weighing on her shoulders.

Reed relaxed a bit. "Look, I can shoot you right now. Or, you can live a little longer stacking a new wall next to that one."

They remained in place, an uneasy silence between them.

Reed rested one arm on his knee. "Your choice, guys, but we don't have all day."

Dawson rallied, a deep breath expanding his chest. He began stacking loose stones next to the "ruin" that held Karl's desiccated body. All Malia could do was stare at Dawson's movements in morbid fascination.

In minutes, Dawson had laid a ring of stones

for the structure, a foundation three feet by six. Large enough for two bodies. He began to add a second layer.

Reed sat back on his haunches, pistol always at the ready.

"So," Dawson stopped for a moment. "Why not just bury our bodies? Why all this work for a stone... container?"

"There's a federal law prevents people from opening up old granaries or removing the walls of pueblo ruins. Once I put a lid on this, it'll take a permit or a court order to let some archaeologist open it up. Buys us a lot more time to be long, long gone. Assuming," he grinned, "they ever find you in the first place."

"Well, then, it won't hurt you to tell us. What happened with the kidnapping? Did it all go sideways on you?"

Reed glared at them. "Yeah, it did. Her old man," he pointed at Malia, "refused to pay up and stopped taking our calls. Your papa," venom in his voice, "doesn't give a flying shit about his little girl."

She knew it couldn't be true about her parents. And now, she was absolutely sure—they'd kidnapped her when they'd meant to take Shiela. They'd been calling Sheila's father for ransom money, money he wasn't going to pay because he knew they didn't have his daughter.

Her own parents had been spared the thought that she had been in danger. Still, here she was, about to become a permanent part of an archeological site.

"Just three of you?" Dawson lifted another stone and turned to place it on the growing wall.

"Yeah," Reed nodded. "But with some help from a local."

Reed watched Dawson, who flinched.

"What did you say?" Dawson asked.

"You heard me. Someone who's known Cooper for years. We wouldn't get far in that hunk of an RV. They got us a stolen car, one that won't be reported 'till we're long gone from here."

"Shit."

"Yeah, it's the shits, huh, deputy?" Reed's grin filled with satisfaction, malevolence etched in the corners of his eyes.

A tap-tapping sound rose from behind Reed, someplace in the pueblo ruins. A row of four rooms had been built along the sheer side of the bluff, a thousand years old. The rooms shared three common walls between them. Four rectangular doorways seemed like monoliths of space, deep and dark, the interiors invisible from outside. The desert sun was heating, baking the bald cliffs above them.

Another tap-tapping sound came from the ancient ruins.

Reed turned to look.

Malia managed to regulate her breathing a little better. Don't think about what comes next, she thought. Concentrate on each breath, each moment of life, and feel it with all your soul.

Tap-tap.

This time, Dawson stopped to look up. Reed rose slowly, keeping his pistol aimed loosely in Malia's direction.

Tap-tap.

Reed stepped toward the ruins. "Cooper? Are you there? What are you doing?"

Malia glanced at Dawson and back at Reed.

Tap-tap-tap-tap.

Reed moved closer to the first room in the row of Pueblo ruins, searching around him, his gaze bouncing from Dawson to Malia to the empty doorway, and back again. "Stay where you are," he told them.

Tap-tap.

Reed pointed his gun at the entrance to the first ruin. "Whoever you are, come out of there!"

Tap.

Reed stepped closer to the doorway, both hands on

the gun, arm straight and stiff, ready to fire.

No more noise came from the old building.

Reed glanced at Malia and Dawson again and moved quickly into the room and out of sight.

Should they run? Could they get away in time? But Malia could hardly stand up, let alone escape from a man with a gun.

In only a moment, Reed came back outside, his pistol lowered, a puzzled look in his eyes.

Just then, a man stepped from the adjacent room, weathered tree branch in his arms, and swung hard against the back of Reed's head, the sound like the crack of a bat on a baseball.

Reed crumpled to the ground.

Relic stood over the man, panting for a moment. He looked at Dawson and Malia and broke into a wide, welcome smile, teeth shining, eyes crinkling in the sunlight.

CHAPTER 68

Relic pulled Dawson's pistol from Reed's belt and held it in the air. "This must be yours."

"How did…?" Dawson said.

"I followed you out of the slot canyon. Had to climb up a ledge when I heard the flash flood coming." Relic grinned.

Dawson flexed his knees and smiled. Malia tucked her legs under her weight and started to stand. Dawson helped her up and they both walked toward Relic.

"You were dead!" Malia moved past Reed and into Relic with a tight hug, squeezing him like an old friend.

"There's a lot of that going 'round." Relic held the pistol away from his body, a dead fish he had no interest in keeping.

Dawson took his pistol and slid it into the holster. He knelt, reached for Reed's neck, and felt for a pulse.

Malia looked up at Relic. "How?"

Dawson put his handcuffs on Reed and took the man's Glock. "I saw you down at the bottom of those cliffs."

"Well," he pulled gently away from Malia. "You saw my shirt, at least." He pointed to the T-shirt he wore and she realized he'd removed his outer layer. "I wrapped it in a rock and tossed it, hoping this ass," he pointed at Reed, "would see it and figure I was still in it. It was quite a ways down the cliff."

They both stared at Relic for a moment.

"What?" he asked.

Malia gave him another bear hug.

"It fooled us, too," Dawson said. "We owe you our lives."

Relic waved away the remark with a half-hearted swat. Malia released her grip on his ribs.

"And this," Dawson turned and wiggled a finger in the hole in the back of his shirt.

"Sorry about your uniform," Relic said.

"My *uniform?* Like I said, we owe you for this," Dawson reached his hand toward Relic and they shook, each man's eyes meeting the other.

Relic released his grip. "I kinda thought you were looking to arrest me."

"Well," Dawson looked at his feet and mumbled. "Maybe I was."

"Not anymore?" Malia asked.

"Not anymore." Dawson grinned. "And now, finally, I have solid proof that you're out here," he waved his arm, "living in these canyons."

Relic frowned.

Dawson continued. "The sheriff thinks you're some kind of ghost, a myth, a figment of my imagination, but now…" his voice trailed off.

Malia watched Relic and said to Dawson: "Maybe we're not so sure just *what we saw*…"

Relic smiled at her.

"Maybe," she added, "maybe you clocked this ass in the head, Dawson. Just now. And Relic's at the bottom of those cliffs somewhere."

Dawson rubbed his forehead with the palm of his hand. "Ah, yes."

"Maybe you poked that hole in your shirt and played dead," she pointed a finger at him.

"Maybe," Dawson said to Malia. "But let's get you out of here now."

Relic pointed at the pickup, thirty yards away. "I ran across a car battery. Thought it was odd until I noticed the hood of your truck raised up like that."

Relic walked from the ruins, across the sandstone base, and into the brush along the arroyo. Malia took Dawson's arm to steady her, and they followed. Several yards away, Relic stopped and pointed down the creek bed. "About another forty yards that way."

Malia suddenly remembered. "Hey, there's two more of those guys."

Relic shook his head. "There was a black pickup when I first got here, when I found you in the old camper. It's not here now. One of them must have taken it out of the canyon."

Dawson nodded. "He's right."

"So, where's the third guy?" she asked, eyes searching.

CHAPTER 69

A plume of red dust spiraled upward from the dirt road, a vehicle storming its way toward the arroyo.

A sheriff's Jeep.

Though it was probably too far for the driver to see, Dawson waved. "It's about time."

"I'll go get the battery," Relic said and trotted away.

The Jeep slowed as it crossed the dry bed and gunned up the other side. The driver must have seen them because it drove straight toward them and Dawson's truck.

The Jeep skidded to a stop a few yards away and Stanovich jumped from the cab.

"What's going on?" Stanovich walked toward Dawson and Malia. "I've been out looking for Karl, but where've you been?"

Dawson raised the palms of his hand, a gesture

meant to quiet Stanovich. "You won't believe it."

"Try me."

"First, this is Malia." Dawson waved toward her. "She's the victim of a kidnapping."

"What?" Stanovich stopped and put his hands on his utility belt.

Dawson explained how he'd come to the canyon searching for Karl when Malia escaped from an old trailer where they'd been keeping her. He said Reed came along, just a hunter who wanted to help, he'd thought, but he was one of the kidnappers.

"Wait! So where is this Reed fellow?" Stanovich asked.

Dawson poked a thumb toward the ruins. "Up there. Handcuffed."

"What else?"

Dawson explained the rest of the story, leaving Relic out of the mix. "So, we've got one more kidnapper, maybe in that fancy RV over there. We need to deal with him right away. But Malia and I are pretty dehydrated."

"Whoa. Right. Yeah," Stanovich stepped back to the Jeep and pulled out two bottles of water. He handed one to Malia, who took long, deep gulps. He walked to Dawson and as the deputy took the water, Stanovich reached neatly into Dawson's holster and removed his pistol.

"What!" Dawson stepped back.

Stanovich raised Dawson's gun at him. "Put the gun you got from Reed on the ground."

"What are you doing?" Dawson took a step toward Stanovich.

Blam!

The bullet grazed Dawson's left shoulder, spinning him full circle and into the dirt.

"Gun on the ground. Now."

Water dribbled down Malia's shirt as she stared at Stanovich. He was the "inside" help that Reed said the kidnappers had used.

Dawson set Reed's gun on the ground, gathered his feet beneath him, and stood straight, hands in the air. A spot of blood the size of a quarter pooled on the edge of his shoulder.

"Now, we're going to get Reed uncuffed and let him finish what he started."

"I can't believe this!" Dawson stammered. "I can't believe you'd do this."

"Yeah, well…Cooper's an old pal. We got our juvey record together, him and me, back in the day. And lending him a hand is a helluva lot more lucrative than that measly salary." His eyes hardened. "Now, back to those ruins, the both of you, slow and easy."

CHAPTER 70

Malia could hardly believe the turn of events. She looked around, searching for something, anything that could help them, but they hadn't been able to radio for help, there was still another kidnapper out there uncuffed, and now a crooked deputy had his gun sights on them.

A patch of grass by the arroyo wiggled in the still air. *Relic?*

She took one step closer to the gun that lay on the ground, the one Dawson had taken from Reed, and began to lower her water bottle to set it down.

Stanovich watched them like a falcon.

There was no way she could reach the gun in time to use it, but she wanted to with all her soul, willing herself to try it, take the risk, how could her situation get any worse?

A stone flew across the way, just behind Stanovich,

who did not seem to notice. Then a second one bounced off his head and he jerked backward, focused on the tall grass now, searching for the person who'd thrown it.

The decision steamed into her brain in an instant, without reservation, without any "what ifs." This was the last time Malia was going to be a victim in this god-awful kidnapping. She reached for Reed's pistol and noticed the cold metal in her hand for a millisecond before she raised it upward and aimed at Stanovich.

Boom!

Stanovich jerked violently backwards, dropping his weapon, stumbling back until he tripped on a rock and fell hard onto his bottom, his eyes wide with shock. His right arm reached for his left shoulder, and he began to moan, a deep, sick groan of pain, his eyes now clamped shut like a vice, his boots scrambling helplessly in the sand.

Dawson quickly grabbed the gun from Malia and aimed it at Stanovich. "Get my gun from him, and his," he said, and Malia slid to the ground and did just that, tossing them aside.

Relic rose from behind the lip in the arroyo, hands in the air, grin on his face.

Dawson rubbed his arm and looked back at Malia. "Get his cuffs from his belt."

Stanovich rocked sideways on his hip, pressing a hand to his shoulder, whining like a toddler. Malia tried once, twice, three times, and finally she got the handcuffs from his belt.

Dawson strode toward them, a soldier in command. He handed Reed's gun back to Malia and shoved Stanovich face first into the dirt.

"Hey, hey," Stanovich complained as Dawson put one cuff on the man's left hand and when he wrenched it back, Stanovich screamed again and again, the sound of fear and terror and impossible pain. Dawson ignored him, cuffing both hands together behind his back.

"Sorry to have to do that," he stepped away from Stanovich. "But I'd say you brought that one on yourself." Dawson wiped the sweat from his brow.

Malia stepped forward and handed Dawson the pistols. He tucked Reed's and Stanovich's into his belt and took his own in his hand.

Relic moved closer to them. "I'm impressed there, sister," he said to Malia. "You defended yourself. You actually shot the guy! And he deserved it."

Her lips parted into a broad smile.

"Looks like you're no victim, anymore."

His words pleased her more than he could know, warmth spreading from her gut and into her arms and up into her ruddy cheeks.

Damn right, she thought.

CHAPTER 71

Fifty yards away, the fancy RV rumbled to life, a puff of gray smoke excreting from the tail pipe.

Dawson began to move toward the RV, but Malia had her hand on his arm, leaning into it. "You'll never reach it in time," she said.

Dawson pulled away from her and ran toward the dirt road, his injured arm dangling by his side, his rhythm ragged, his gait uneven. The RV rolled quickly toward the road, beating Dawson to the junction, where it turned away from them.

The deputy closed in faster, nearing the rear of the massive vehicle and it looked like he might catch it after all when it dipped into the arroyo, speeding downward and almost out of sight.

Dawson kept going for several more yards, but stopped at the edge of the arroyo, hands on his knees, panting.

The RV sped across the bottom of the dry creek bed and up the other side then labored higher up the road until it leveled out. From there, the road lay in a straight line for several miles, a steep cliff dropping off on the left side. They watched as the lumbering canister rocked along, rising, growing smaller each minute.

"Damn it," Dawson forced the words through his teeth.

The RV clutched into higher gear, the engine straining.

Relic adjusted the pack on his back. Dawson raised his hand, shielding his eyes from the sun.

A low, deep, *boom* echoed up the canyon.

The RV lurched and swerved, red dust rising from its sliding tires. A cord of black smoke billowed from the undercarriage, braiding into the air. They could just see a man jump from the driving cab, running away from it, arms flailing.

The RV began to coast backwards, the rear of the colossus headed right for the rim and then it sped straight off the edge, downward onto a ragged shelf, which flipped it one full circle in the air before it struck the ground again, flames bursting from the engine and engulfing the blackened motor home.

The sound reached them a second later: *Boom…Ba boom!*

Relic nodded and turned to walk away.

Malia spun toward him. "You know what happened?"

"Just a loose wire in the engine compartment," Relic said. "And some gas and dry cheat grass for a fire starter."

"When did you do that?" she asked.

"Before sunup. You guys were probably sleeping."

She leapt forward and hugged him again.

Dawson stood where he was for a moment, stunned.

Relic wiggled free, gently stepping back. "Best get that battery into the truck. Radio for help."

Dawson turned and walked back to Malia. They hobbled close to the deputy's truck, and she leaned against the front fender. Dawson went to where Relic had placed the battery. Dawson carried it to the truck, his uninjured arm carrying most of the weight. He slid it onto the base and reconnected the terminals.

Relic said, "Well, friends, let's not do that again anytime soon."

Malia smiled.

Relic began a casual walk toward the arroyo. "Best of luck to you!"

"Wait. You can't go now..." Malia reached toward him.

He waved, turned to go into the dry creek bed and raised two fingers in the air, the universal sign for "peace." In moments, he'd disappeared past the rim.

They stood for a while, breathing the silence.

Malia watched where he'd gone, thinking about all that Sasquatch had shown her high on those sheer cliffs, out across the plateau, under the Milky Way. The spires, domes, hoodoos, pinnacles, banded spires. She remembered when she'd first seen him, a dusty, wiry guy with a goatee and a ponytail. She'd pegged him as some sort of weirdo, a lonely, anti-social, hippie-hermit.

God was she ever wrong.

Never judge a book by its cover, she thought. She glanced at her own clothes, pant legs frayed, waistband wet and torn, her blouse a Rorschach test of smeared grass, blotched dust, and swirling bands of dried sweat. She laughed.

Dawson opened the door to the truck and reached for the radio microphone.

"Mayday, mayday, this is Dawson. Speak to me!"

The radio crackled. "Dispatch here. Where the hell are you?"

"Star Chart Ruins. Send medical help and reinforcements. There're two kidnappers here and one victim. One kidnapper is in my custody. The other should be somewhere along the road to the highway, walking."

"Kidnappers?"

"Yeah. Can you get the sheriff on the radio for me?"

"I can try."

"Stanovich…" he stumbled over how to say it. "Stanovich has been helping the kidnappers."

"Please say again."

He repeated the message.

"You'd better be damn sure about that."

"Sadly, I am. Confession from one of the kidnappers. Then, Stanovich tried to take us back to the kidnapper to have him kill us."

"What?"

"He pulled his gun on us."

"*Shit*. I mean, shoot."

"Tell the sheriff ASAP."

"You got it. I mean 'copy that.' Dispatch out."

CHAPTER 72

Teddy backed up the hill, straining to see behind him as he went, the little Ford bucking against rocks and ruts. When he thought he was high enough up the slope, he shifted into park and slid out of the Escort.

He'd hitched a ride out of the Utah desert then found a used car lot south of Moab, the least reputable one he could find. He'd made up a story about being stranded, his brother sending him cash, and all of that. He was sure the salesman didn't believe him, but the man played along because he needed a sale, and that was good enough for Teddy. He'd spent twelve hundred dollars on the old Ford station wagon, a hundred and ten thousand miles on it, but it ran all right and he had no intention of filing the title or buying license plates or insurance. He'd driven 2,340 miles on the temporary tag in the back window. He'd napped on back roads at night, drank gas station coffee, and ate burritos and candy bars all the way to the outskirts of Kendall, Florida. From there, he'd found this back road into the swamps.

He pulled a sack with two bottles of water and Snickers from the back seat and set it on the ground. He laid a rock against the accelerator, just enough to keep the engine running smoothly, and wrapped a plastic bag on the shifter, something to let him put it in gear without reaching too far into the car. He was going to have to pull his hand away quickly.

Teddy glanced around, making sure he was alone.

He tugged hard on the bag, shifting the car into drive, and spun away as the Escort gathered speed down the hill, the driver side door banging against its frame, the tires guided by ruts in the road. The Ford sped faster and faster and nearly leapt across the paved road at the bottom, bouncing across the macadam and down a slope on the other side, grill-first into the dark, still water, standing on its front bumper for a suspenseful moment. Then the car slid farther into the swamp, its rear splashing hard, bubbles rising from its frame as it slowly sank into the murk and muck, engine dead, cab filling with water and leaves and other debris. Within two minutes, the whole vehicle had been swallowed by the Florida swamp, nothing left but a thin slick of oil.

Teddy picked up the bag of water and candy and meandered back the way he'd driven in, heading to that warm Atlantic Ocean, salty breezes, palm trees, bikini-clad co-eds. What he needed now was a shot of fine whiskey, maybe a fishing boat, and a long, low hammock.

****

Hanna hiked a long, rutted road through the pines, the sweetened scent an integral part of the thin Montana air.

She was exhausted. Her cell phone was at the bottom of a creek that wandered at the edge of the Manning's estate. She'd bought a bus ticket under another name that took her all the way to Bozeman. Last night, she slept on a park bench by the river. She'd decided not to tell her sister she was coming. Best to keep as quiet as possible, spend only cash, avoid hotels.

Cooper had turned out to be a dome-headed man with mush for brains. He'd kidnapped the wrong damn girl, could she believe it? She shook her head again, wondering why she kept falling for dumb asses like him.

Carly would know what to do. She'd help her stay low, rest up, get back on her feet. Get a good new I.D.

She looked up the winding path. Memory had gotten her this far, but there was a fork in the road she hadn't recalled. Which way was her sister's place? Right, or left?

The rumble of an engine reached her ears. She moved quickly off the road and into a strand of choke-cherry bushes, watching. A battered blue Suburban turned the corner, its suspension rising and falling as it climbed over rocks and ruts.

Carly!

Hanna jumped from the brush, waving her arms. The vehicle stopped. Her sister stepped from the SUV, her face a mixture of annoyance and surprise.

"Hanna?"

The two of them embraced, Carly blurting a string of questions, Hanna talking over her, both of them happy to be together again.

"Wait, stop." Carly held up her hands. "Get in."

Hanna slid into the front seat, finally relaxed, finally feeling at home.

CHAPTER 73

It had been days but felt like only a few hours since Sheriff Leavitt had come to Slickrock Canyon to get her and Dawson and to pick up Reed, Cooper, and former deputy Stanovich. She'd dropped her classes at the business school in Los Angeles and planned to live on the tuition refund for a month or two in the little town where the sheriff's office roosted. She'd begun the search for a job, something, anything, temporary or—who knew? Maybe something permanent.

She'd asked Dawson to take her back to the "scene of the crime," ostensibly so she could refresh her memory, but the truth was that her memory needed no refreshing at all. In fact, her memory needed a break. Maybe a twenty-year break. But Sheriff Leavitt approved the request and she and Dawson wandered the Star Chart Ruins for nearly an hour, ducking their heads into the empty doorways, scanning the rock art, pondering the solstice markings and the midnight map of stars in the summer sky. Wondering what the people here must have been like; farming corn, beans, squash, keeping domesticated turkeys and dogs, studying the black of night, dreaming what life on this earth might be all about. Like she was doing.

They kept a lookout for Relic, but he did not reappear. Maybe because she wasn't trapped in a decrepit pull-behind trailer, screaming her lungs off.

They sat together on a ledge in front of the ruins.

"This is a long way from the social life of L.A." Malia pointed around them.

Dawson nodded. "Must be a pretty radical change from there to these slot canyons. Ancient ruins and astro-maps."

"Flash floods." Her eyes grew wide.

"Right," he nodded.

"Snakes." She wrinkled her nose.

"Yeah, *one* snake, anyway."

"Well, and not to mention the whole kidnapping thing."

His smile seemed to warm the air. "Yeah, that's right, and the whole kidnapping thing. But it did get you out to see this red rock country."

She wrapped her arm around his and touched her head to his shoulder, a quick, sideways hug. "Thank you again for all that you did to help me out here." When she straightened, she thought she saw him blush.

He dusted his pants and stood. She did the same.

Dawson walked ahead of her, examining the flats and the arroyo that led farther up the canyon. She moved in front of the ruins near the mother-in-law suite and sat again, her muscles still a little stiff.

Hospital staff had checked her for broken bones and internal injuries and declared her to be all in one piece. She'd called her folks from there. Because the kidnappers thought they had taken her friend Shiela, no one had called Malia's parents with any kind of ransom demand. They wondered why they hadn't heard from her in a few days but hadn't been worried.

She realized she'd been more than a little blinded by Sheila—the glitz, jewelry, fashions, nightclubs. They'd both been chasing greed, as Relic called it; a race no one can win, keeping their minds busy with busyness and self-importance. Sheila was completely into it all, as a lifestyle, even.

Dawson was right. It took something radical to change her perspective. If she hadn't been kidnapped by that bunch of idiots, she never would have left L.A., never would have seen this magnificent country, its spires, cliffs, gorges and mesas. She never would have met Mae, the deer that came to them one night and looked her right in the eyes. A "wild" animal, curious about a human. And Relic, a "wild" moonshining recluse, a desert sasquatch, also an inquisitive creature.

Relic said our thinking is what channels our actions, our futures. And surprises, like the ones she'd had over the last few days, can completely readjust our thinking. It had certainly readjusted hers.

She owed those kidnapping idiots a lot.

The county coroner had taken Karl's body back to the morgue.

The FBI had picked up Reed, Cooper, and Stanovich, right out of the county jail. They were still looking for the third kidnapper, someone Cooper called "Teddy," but they said they had a good lead in Texas.

The FBI had interviewed Sheila, of course, and her mother and stepfather. The feds suspected that someone named Hanna, an employee of a house-cleaning service, may have been feeding inside information to the kidnappers. She'd run away when Sheila returned home, a guilty conscience if there ever was one. She'd left the Manning's mansion and disappeared, but authorities were on the hunt.

Dawson was heralded as a hero in the local press, and he deserved every bit of it. Talk was growing that he ought to run for sheriff when Leavitt retires at the end of his term. Dawson wasn't sure, and his brand of humility was a breath of fresh air. In fact, he'd been a surprise to her in more ways than one. She was looking forward to dinner with him at a little micro-brew place called the Sweetwater Station.

The police dispatcher—a wonderful lady—helped her get a fresh set of clothes. More practical, too. Jeans, button-up shirts, wool socks, hiking boots. And a "Leavitt for Sheriff" campaign hat from the old bear's last run for office.

After talking it through with Dawson, she confirmed the key source of the kidnapper's mistake. She and Sheila were roughly the same height and were both brunettes with short haircuts, but the real kicker was the ultra-white shawl that Sheila gave to Malia to keep while Sheila went to the dance floor. In all that neon light, the shawl was florescent, making facial features hard to see. The kidnappers had thought Sheila was still wearing the shawl when they'd drugged Malia. They must have figured it out eventually, when Sheila's father ignored the ransom calls. But by that point, they had only one option left: kill her and Dawson. If it hadn't been for Relic, they'd both be dead.

Dawson walked closer to the arroyo, taking pictures of the ruined camper that now rested upside down at the bottom.

She hadn't patted her pocket in search of her phone since she'd returned. Any call she had to make, she'd made from the hotel room or the sheriff's office. She'd kicked it. Eventually, she'd probably get another "smart" phone, but her days of watching or playing on it for hours on end were over. For a while, at least.

She took a deep breath and stared across the canyon at a vanilla—colored spire, a lone sentinel guarding a massive set of glistening, sandstone cliffs. A thicket of brush lay above the dry creek bed, an eyebrow on the lazy rim. An autumn breeze clattered dry cottonwood leaves like castanets.

She'd gone from one whole world into another. Now that she'd seen this one, how could she ever leave it?

AUTHOR'S NOTE AND ACKNOWLEDGEMENTS

Thank you for reading *Slickrock* – I really hope you enjoyed it! As an author, I depend heavily on book reviews and referrals. If you think others might enjoy the novel, too, please leave a quick review on Amazon or any other internet site you use for selecting books to read. *The moment it takes to leave a quick book rating makes a lasting difference for the author!*

Hats off to my lovely and patient wife for all her support while working on this effort. Thanks to her, Dad, and Sarah, for their valued insights and edits. Special thanks to Buck T. and Ron S. for their friendship and their editorial help with the story line and the many details I needed to keep straight! Thanks to all my friends, family, and colleagues, whose support helped keep my head above water.

Thanks to my talented son Nate for the wonderful map art!

I also thank Daniel Thiede for his beautiful cover art and book design and his much-needed help with the technical aspects of the work.

Thanks to all who understand our kinship with the planet and those who work in the service of their ideals.

BROKEN INN

"Well, butter my buns…"

He shaded his eyes with the palm of his hand.

There were two pickup trucks in Demon's Roost canyon – one in the deep arroyo at the base of sheer cliffs to the south, one on the upper flats that made up most of the corkscrew canyon. There'd been uranium mining here in the 1950s, but what these yahoos were doing now was a mystery.

Relic tightened his ponytail and stared into the twisting gorge.

Yesterday morning, snow capped the hoodoos – white icing on scarlet cupcakes. By this afternoon, the sun-fired rocks had begun radiating heat near 100 degrees, wringing moisture from the human body like a twisted sponge. The cliffs above him seemed to glow, slivers of clay injected into the blood-red sandstone like fat marbled into raw steak. A pair of crows squawked overhead.

An unlikely descendent of disparate clansmen – one Scottish, one Hopi – Relic wandered these plateaus and chasms, a sometimes-trespasser, recluse, and moonshiner. He'd been called a vagabond, a sasquatch of the desert, but these remote places were home.

He left his pack by a rock and trotted down the trail to the bottom of the canyon. He moved quickly around the first bend to a spot close to the truck on the flats. No one seemed to be around. He walked to the pickup, a silver double-cab, its tailgate down. Topographic maps lay flattened across the truck bed, rocks on the corners to hold them in place. An empty five-gallon container for water sat on the end of the tailgate, neon-orange stripes across its side. A gust of wind slid the plastic canister off the edge and Relic picked it up.

The maps were of Demon's Roost and places to the north. Scribbles and circles were penciled over the contour lines, but he couldn't tell what they meant. The second truck, the one in the dry creek bed, sat around a bend in the canyon, out of sight from this position.

Something made him uneasy. Some distant vibration, maybe. The crows had gone silent. Charcoal clouds hung in the east.

Two men rounded the corner, boots rasping over the sand, heads down, mumbling to each other. He watched from behind the silver truck, some fifteen feet above them and thirty yards away. One wore jeans and a white dress shirt, out of place in this remote canyon. The other wore a red shirt with a leather strap across his shoulder.

Relic took a step back and felt it again – this time a deep rumble under his boots – and suddenly he knew what was coming. Though desperately dry, it was water that had shaped these desert lands, sheer bluffs and jagged drainages wrought by the power of rain. A cloudburst 50 miles away could become a flash flood in these narrow canyons, a deadly blast of water exploding with little warning. The men in the arroyo stood directly in its path.

"Hey, hey!" Relic raised the empty water container above his head, waving it in the air, sprinting past the pickup truck and toward the edge of the ravine.

One of the men looked up.

"Get out of there! Out of there!" Relic shouted, pointing up the embankment, urging them to run from the dry creek bed before it was too late.

The other man straightened, suddenly startled, and reached for his side.

"Flash flood! Flash flood!" Relic waved the plastic canister again and stepped to the edge of the ravine.

The dissonance in his toes became a bellow in his head, an angry groan.

One man began to climb from the bottom of the arroyo, boots slipping up the sandy rise. The other lifted his hand from his side, a pistol in his fingers, aiming it toward Relic.

Relic spiraled backward reflexively, stepping suddenly into thin air, dropping down the slope, skidding feet-first through loose sand all the way to the bottom. He stood and looked at the gunman, who'd holstered his pistol and begun climbing the side of the arroyo behind his companion. In a moment, they both stood above the empty drainage, out of danger.

Now the sound of thunder rolled through the canyon, echoes doubling the alarm. Relic ran down the dry bed, frantically searching its steep walls for a place he could ascend. The rumble became the roar of whitewater, ramjet engines at full throttle, all other sound blasted aside by the urgency and enormity of the coming flood.

Relic turned in time to see a two-foot bank of water rise behind him, precursor to the deluge to come.

He held tight to the empty container and ran toward the spot the two men had used to climb from the dry bed, but as he began to scramble up the slope, the coffee-colored water, heavy with silt, reached his feet, sweeping them forward, twisting him down into the roiling river.

He wrapped his arms around the canister, his make-shift life vest, and lifted his feet in front of him. A surge forced him underwater – his eyes closed, mouth shut – then lifted him rapidly toward the top of the arroyo, shoving him forward faster than a man could run. He kicked to keep his feet downstream, buffers against rocks, trees, or cliffs. The newborn river hurtled him around the bend, a choleric infant wailing at the world.

The second pickup truck lay directly in his path.

He wiggled and twisted, paddling his boots as fast as he could, but the truck came swiftly closer, closer, his feet about to smash into the rear window. If he were forced through the glass and into the cab of the truck, the river would pin him there and drown him. But as he approached, he seemed to slow, then slow some more. His boots touched the window. He bent his knees and pushed away, then he realized he hadn't slowed at all. The truck had been lifted from the ground and shoved forward with him. The water carried them both through the flood together.

The deluge raged around another bend in the canyon, rocks clacking violently against each other along the bottom, tumbling into the flow from the sides, debris that could crush him in a second if he got caught between them. The truck separated from him, rolling to its side. A wave suddenly tossed his head and chest above the flow, his feet pulled downward. He flipped forward and under the rapids, no time to take a breath. Despite the buoyancy of the canister, the swirling river forced him downward, somersaulting into the dark. He lost all sense of direction, what was up or down, dizzy in the swirling storm, helpless under the unyielding, raging current. Pressure rose in his lungs to near explosion, his diaphragm tensing, preparing to blow his final breath from his chest, when finally he spun upward, his head breaking through, and he gasped.

He pushed on the container, lifting his head as high as he could, hungrily sucking in air. The sides of the arroyo sped by, bending left, then right, disorienting him. His boots struck something hard, and he realized his legs were dangling below him again – a dangerous position. He pulled himself into a back float, feet downstream, arms clutching the canister. Waves splashed into his eyes and mouth, blinding him for seconds at a time, forcing him to take quick, shallow breaths. The current threatened to spin him again, so he paddled his feet, twisting to keep his face above water.

The waves began to spread farther apart and his sight improved when he squinted. The truck was behind him now, spinning slowly in the current as he passed another bend in the gorge.

The sky seemed to lighten as the canyon walls receded. He felt his elevation lower as the flood spread across more open ground, closer to its destination in the

Colorado River.

He spun to his left and kicked as hard as he could, moving out of the current. In moments, his bottom touched hard ground. He pushed farther away from the receding water until he could sit up. A three-inch flow continued to swirl around him, but he knew he was safe.

He took full, deep breaths, clearing the adrenaline from his system, regaining a sense of balance.

The flow of water slowly turned to mud. The truck had rounded the last corner, then gotten stuck behind a rock and buried nearly a foot deep in the sandy bottom. He dropped the empty container and wiped the water and hair from his eyes.

"This is the worst thing that's happened since the last thing," he told himself with a grin. It was the second time he'd been caught in a flash flood and nearly drowned. The first time, it'd been his own damn fault. Well, hell, he thought, maybe it was his own fault this time, too.

If the swim hadn't been so deadly, part of him, at least, could have admitted to the thrill.

He sat for a moment, staring into the clear sky. Who were those guys and what the hell were they doing in this canyon? And why did one of them draw his pistol when he'd warned them about the flood?

"I guess no good deed goes unpunished," he scolded himself. He stood slowly, shaking out his arms and legs. He removed his shirt, wrung it out, and put it back on. "I'll dry you out later," he spoke to his pants and boots.

It was time to get the hell out of there.

The tent became a dome of light, then began to smolder and burst into flame near the back, near the kitchen stove.

"Hey, we just cleaned the grill back there," Relic said, making Wyatt laugh.

The fire spread slowly, casting a halo of light across the camp. Security guards hollered, workers yelled their curses and questions, and everyone rushed to see what the commotion was all about.

"Is she really crazy enough to do that?" Wyatt asked.

"Yep," Relic nodded.

"Well, shee-it," Wyatt did his best imitation of Faye.

Relic smiled. "Don't let her hear you or she'll knock your block off."

"No doubt."

"Would you see what you can do to slow down that backhoe up ahead of us and anything else with a lock and key? Then work your way north, swing back toward the staircase and we can meet up there."

Wyatt nodded.

"Keep a close look out. They'll be searching as soon as the mess is under control."

"What's your next move?" Wyatt asked.

Relic jerked his thumb toward the portable toilets.

"Really?" Wyatt said.

Relic turned and faded into the dark. Wyatt heard footfalls, someone moving quickly toward him. After a moment, he recognized her shape bobbing along. She tossed something and he heard it clacking into the bed of a pickup. She nearly ran into him.

"Hey." He put his hands out toward her.

"Hey," she said, slowing, but only a bit. "Here." She tossed a stick of dynamite to him, the fuse sparkling lit.

"Shit!"

"Throw it!" she shouted as she ran past. "Now!"

Wyatt stared at the tube in his hand. The fuse sputtered and spat and shortened with every second, time compressed with the tightness of his breath, the glowing fuse moving forward immutably until something like a spinning clutch popped in his chest and muscle movement became possible again. He reached his arm back and threw it as far and as fast as he could, then he spun and ran to the side of another truck and turned back to look.

The pickup Faye had tossed something into rose into the air with a smack that washed away all other sound, then fell back to the ground with a nasty twist as pieces of sheet metal dropped from the sky.

"Holy…"

Wyatt's stick of dynamite exploded somewhere beyond another truck, lighting something on fire, sending a second sonic boom through his skull, making him jump in his tracks. He stared at the blaze as it settled into a steady burn and looked the direction Faye had run.

A third, fourth, and fifth explosion erupted in quick succession in the row of portable toilets and Wyatt knew it was Relic's work. Where was Relic's peaceful resistance now? Lord, he hoped no one was in those toilets. Then, he thought, what a mess of shit, and he giggled and smacked his hands together.

Oh, my god, was it possible to have so much fun? He never expected stopping Lord Winnieship from stealing this canyon to feel so damn good.

He stared at the fire he'd started and tried to think. He wanted to follow Faye but there was no telling what other mayhem she had in mind, and he did not want to walk into an exploding outhouse. He tried to regulate his breathing, with only a little luck. He circled away from the path Faye had taken, giving her a wide berth, moving to the outer edge of the parked vehicles.

Wyatt turned and trotted toward a lone backhoe, maybe sixty yards away. Though the electric lights of the compound were out, the kitchen and dining room blaze cast a sallow glow on the tops of the other tents and equipment. The upper arm of the yellow backhoe was lit like a candle.

His shins scraped across brittle sage and he slowed to a walk. He'd lost his own toothpicks, so that trick would not work with the heavy equipment. After Faye's dynamite, toothpicks seemed pretty pathetic anyway. Maybe there was a set of keys kept in the ignition that he could toss away. Or maybe he could flatten its tires or pull wires from under the dash to disable the beast. He turned to watch the bobbing of flashlights all around the burning mess tent a quarter of a mile away. The voices of men rose and fell in a rhythm that was almost musical, like an offbeat composition.

He stopped at the base of the backhoe and stared up at the top, where the boom and dipper attached. He circled the machine to the open cabin and peered inside.

"Stop and turn around." The voice was deep and familiar.

Wyatt turned and raised his hands. Even in the semi-dark, Lynch's muscled bulk identified him immediately. He held a pistol aimed at Wyatt's chest.

"You!" Lynch said. "You sonofabitch."

Wyatt saw the left hook a milli-second before it struck his jaw, wrenching his head away and toward the ground. He stumbled to the side. A blow to his stomach struck like a rocket and his chest ached, all the veins in his body shut down by a sonic boom. Slivers of light flashed through his eyes, closed tight against the assault. He sensed himself floating to the earth, his muscles turned to liquid. He was out before he hit the dirt.

Excerpt from
WINGS OVER GHOST CREEK

He sucked a shallow breath of air, pulled his gaze from the dead arm, and looked back the way he'd come. From this perspective, the arm was well-hidden on the backside of the long pile of dirt, tucked close to the low rock face and well out of view from the hangar and the tents beyond. Last night's heavy storm had flushed loose soil from the canyon slopes and probably from the body, too. He tried not to look back at the fragile hand, but he couldn't help himself. Skin shriveled against the tiny bones, stiff leather holding the assembly of joints together, keeping the fingers pointed in confusing, haphazard directions, their owner not sure which way to go. Red nail polish added a cheap party flare, a celebration completely out of place.

Holy eff. Hold it together, he told himself, get back to camp and pretend he'd never seen it. Tell Thomas. No one else. Someone here could have killed this girl, must have killed her. Why? What had happened here?

He turned his eyes to his feet and shuffled across the ground, moving to the edge of the pile of dirt. He peered around the mound and saw the edge of the hangar and the back of the tents. No one seemed to be around, so he hustled away from the dirt, across the hard-packed surface, and into the hangar. He went to the yellow plane again and leaned on the right strut, his breath still shallow and labored.

Owen looked beyond the hangar to the field outside and the Cessna waiting for them. Where was Thomas?

"Did you get that cold drink?"

Panic charged through his brain, a devil's hot wire crackling from one ear to the other. His head jerked toward the front of the plane and he clamped his hands tightly on the strut. Everett's question was smooth but – was there an undertone in his voice?

Owen managed to force a breath.

"No..." he patted the wing support, glanced at Everett, then spoke to the plane itself, too nervous to look at the man again. Squeezing the strut helped him to focus. "I got sidetracked by this old Aeronca. What year is it, do you know?"

"1946, I'm told."

"Oh."

"Are you a pilot?" Everett moved out of the sunlight and into the shade of the hangar. Owen knew the man could see him better now.

"No, no, I'm not. Tried to take some lessons, but..." He struggled to keep his thoughts on the aircraft, away from what he'd discovered. "Just look at this panel, the instrument panel," he pointed. "Not hardly any instruments here, though. It's all metal, too, like the dashboards on old cars." He kept his eyes on the cockpit, still reluctant to look directly at Everett.

"Yeah, I've looked it over myself." Everett's voice seemed more normal now, more conversational. "The owner has a friend who came out here a couple of days ago. He's restoring the old bird, but I don't know how far he's gotten. The fabric looks like a stiff breeze would pull it off." He ran his hand across the edge of the wing opposite Owen. "You wouldn't catch me flying in this death trap." Everett wandered away from the plane, plucked a long blade of grass from the ground and began to twist it absentmindedly.

"Yeah, the cloth on this one needs completely replaced." Owen tried to sound like an authority on the subject and felt his nerves calm a little as he spoke. He ducked under the wing and walked into the sunlight. "Seen my boss?"

"I think he's about done," Everett pointed toward the tents along Ghost Creek. Thomas and Angela were walking slowly back toward the Cessna. Angela was explaining something, Thomas nodding.

"Well, it was nice meeting you." Everett moved

quickly toward Owen and offered his hand, his smile show-room friendly, his shake cold and curt.

"Yes. Nice meeting you, too." Owen made eye contact briefly and turned back toward the Cessna. "Better get going."

He strode toward the rented Park Service plane, muscle memory moving his legs, thoughts flowing back to that tortured hand, its ragged movement in the breeze. He tried to be nonchalant about getting the hell out of there. Angela and Thomas came closer to the Cessna.

"Got what we need?" Owen asked Thomas.

Thomas looked up. "Yep. Thanks for the tour and good luck to you," he said to Angela. He shook hands with her and Everett and turned back to the plane.

Owen did not wait to be told to climb in. He adjusted his seatbelt, put the headset on, and waited. Thomas did the same.

How was he going to tell Thomas about the dead girl's arm? When should he tell him? Angela and Everett positioned themselves to one side and in front of the Cessna. They could see any conversation between him and Thomas, so he stayed quiet.

Thomas spent a moment examining the air map and checking the instruments. Out of the corner of his eye, Owen saw the man with the red hat, Luke, run up to

Everett and whisper urgently in his ear. Everett glared at the plane, then gave some sort of order to Luke, who ran out of view. Did they know he'd found the girl's body?

"Clear prop!" Thomas pumped the throttle and turned the key, the engine spitting to life. Owen sat back in his seat, eyes straight ahead, and listened to the engine as Thomas adjusted the fuel mixture and checked the magnetos, turning first one off, then the other, then both back on for flight, Owen wishing he would hurry the hell up. Thomas finally pushed the throttle forward and the engine roared, the Cessna shuddered, and they began to roll down the dirt strip, vibrating, bouncing, jarring over small ruts until suddenly, liftoff, and the ride became smooth and even, the engine solid and throaty, clear air ahead of them, and Owen finally took a deep breath.

Thomas made a gentle turn to their left, flying back toward the creek, the dig site, and the old hangar, circling to gain altitude needed to fly over the plateau above the camp. They rose steadily as they went, Owen thinking how to explain what he'd found, hoping he'd done the right thing by waiting until they were in the air, bound for home base.

They leveled out about two miles past the Quonset hut, aiming for the broad Colorado River as they continued to climb beyond the canyon. A ribbon of dust rose to their right, a truck in motion along the road, soon to be well behind them. Ghost Creek faded from view as they neared the level of the plateau. They could see the bronze river beyond as it wound its way southward, on toward the Grand Canyon, on to the Gulf of California. Owen rubbed his hands on his pants and readied himself.

"Thomas," he spoke into the microphone on his headset.

"Yes?"

"I've got something to tell you, something I discovered down there while you were with the archeologist..."

"Yes?" Thomas checked his GPS and adjusted his heading.

Just then, a hollow thump jarred Thomas forward and he pushed the yoke in, then tugged and released it as he slumped back in his seat. Owen grabbed the yoke and his eyes swelled wide and he stared at Thomas' slackened face and began to scream his name, bobbing the plane's nose up, down, up, when another hollow thump jarred them and oil sprayed into the air and onto the right side of the windshield and he heard the motor cough, and cough again, and felt the Cessna lose its power, dropping in the air, descending toward the ground and he screamed again.

DIAMONDS OF DEVIL'S TAIL

"Wicked chickens lay deviled eggs, but this one's rotten, too." Relic took the binoculars from his eyes and stroked his buffalo-beard goatee. Something about the man on the trail below made his skin tingle.

He slid away from the edge, out of the man's line of sight, and looked about. An unlikely descendant from clans of the Hopi and Scottish, Relic wandered the remote reaches of the Green and Colorado Rivers and the high plateaus between them, a weathered hermit at home in the desert outback, roaming ancient trails, brewing his homemade gin at a couple of narrow, spring-fed crags tucked above the floodplains. He tightened his ponytail, errant strands of white flashing through his coal-black hair.

A dried-out branch of cottonwood leaned against the nearest in a row of six Pueblo houses nestled tightly between the floor and ceiling of the cliff, a string of separate rooms, their stone blocks still mortared together in the corners. Inside were mano stones, held in the hand for grinding corn, and metate, wide-bottom slabs used for the same purpose. A child's bow and arrow, chert for making knives and arrowheads, and bowls of corn, squash, and other seeds were set neatly on indoor ledges under a layer of dust; their owners, it seemed, only away for the winter. In the farthest room was a row of large pots painted with white and black bolts of lightning, edges curved and sharp, with handles on their sides, tops still sealed tight, their contents a thousand year-old mystery. Relic meant to keep it that way.

He leaned forward again. The man strode purposefully toward the high cliff with something long, something strangely out of place, glinting in the desert sun. He put the binoculars back to his eyes.

Of all the things to be lugging in this remote country, to be balancing on bony shoulders in the noonday heat, that angular, outrageous shape was an aluminum ladder, designed for the suburban handyman.

"Well, shit on a shingle." Relic tucked the binoculars away, lay flat near the ruins, and waited.

The man struggled awkwardly up the trail, finally dragging the extension ladder to a stop at the base of the sandstone cliff. He wiped the sweat from his forehead and gazed upward at the solid, sloping rock and the extreme measures the Pueblo people had taken to keep their houses and granaries hidden and safe, high in the cliffs and crags, deep in the desert outback. Centuries ago, they carried masonry, mortar, and jars of water up rickety, wooden ladders to build these solid structures; hard, hot work with just one purpose – protection against interlopers. Now the man below had a ladder of his own, and he rested it against the stone and tugged on the rope that extended it upward, the arms squealing in their tracks, each rung clunking into place as it went.

The man shifted an empty duffle bag across his shoulders and began climbing carefully, one step at a time.

The twenty-eight foot ladder shifted suddenly an inch to the side, but it seemed to find a new, more solid base. The man flexed his knees, testing to make sure the aluminum would not slide any farther, and glanced up. The top of the ladder reached just above the lip of the sandstone ledge.

That man must think he'll find a load of artifacts up here, Relic thought, maybe even lower them to the ground by rope from the ruins, then step back down the ladder unencumbered. But the ancient Pueblo had one last line of defense.

Relic rolled away from the ruins and shifted along the ledge until he was directly in front of the top rung of the ladder, waiting. He listened as the man placed one hand on the step above him, then the next, one at a time, rising cautiously higher.

The man reached the cap of the ledge, but when he looked across the level shelf, where the stone walls rested, there, alone in the red dust, sat Relic looking, he knew, like a weathered Pueblo man, a ghost of the ruins, with a black goatee and a ponytail, holding a three foot cottonwood branch as thick as his arm.

"Shit!" the man's foot slid off one rung and down to the next. "Holy mother…who the hell are you?"

Relic's dark eyes squinted, his lips rose at the corners, and he slid the branch toward the man's ladder.

"What the hell?" the man tightened his grip.

Relic placed the branch on the top rung and began to push.

"No! Shit, no!" He raised his hand for a flash then returned it to the ladder. "You'll kill me!"

Relic slowly pushed the ladder away from the ledge, forcing it to twist outward on one end, then the other, as it lifted from the face of the cliff.

The man dropped both feet to the lower rung and slid his hands quickly down the aluminum sides, dropping his feet, holding for a moment, dropping, holding, dropping as the ladder leaned farther and farther away from the cliff, more and more upright above, ready to catapult him into a pile of rocks, and just as his feet hit the dirt the ladder tipped past its balance, dipped overhead and spun out of his hands and onto the rocky ground with a clang, a bounce, and another clang!

Sign up for book anouncements and special deals at:
AWBALDWIN.COM

Also available from Award Winning Author
A. W. Baldwin:

AN "ENGAGING ACTION...MYSTERY" - READERS' FAVORITE
A.W. BALDWIN
DESERT GUARDIAN
ADVENTURE WRITERS
AWARD WINNING AUTHOR
A RELIC NOVEL

A moonshining hermit.
A campus bookworm.
A midnight murder.

Ethan's world turns upside-down when he slips off the edge of red-rock cliffs into a world of twisting ravines and coveted artifacts. Saved by a mysterious desert recluse named Relic, Ethan must join a whitewater rafting group and make his way back to civilization. But someone in the gorge is killing to protect their illegal dig for ancient treasures... When Anya, the lead whitewater guide, is attacked, he must divert the killer into the dark canyon night, but his most deadly pursuer is not who he thinks... Ethan struggles to save his new friends, face his own mortality, and unravel the chilling murders. But when they flee the secluded canyon, a lethal hunter is hot on their trail…

Can an unlikely duo and a whitewater crew save themselves and an ancient Aztec battlefield from deadly looters?

Readers' Favorite says:
Desert Guardian is an "engaging action… mystery"

The novel features "tough, credible characters"

Readers' Favorite Five Star Review

Buy now from a bookstore near you or amazon.com

"A CAPTIVATING JOYRIDE...A GEM OF A READ" – DIRK CUSSLER
A.W. BALDWIN
RAPTOR CANYON
GRANDMASTER AWARD FINALIST
A RELIC NOVEL

A moonshining hermit.
A big-city lawyer.
A $35million con job.

An impromptu murder leads a hermit named Relic to an unlikely set of dinosaur petroglyphs and to swindlers using the unique rock art to turn the canyon into a high-end tourist trap. Attorney Wyatt and his boss travel to the site to approve the next phase of financing, but his boss is not what he seems... When a treacherous security chief tries to kill Relic, Wyatt is caught in the deadly chase. The mismatched pair must tolerate each other while fleeing through white-water rapids, remote gorges, and hidden caverns. Relic devises a plan to save the treasured canyon, but Wyatt must come to terms with the cost to his career if he fights his powerful boss... A college student with secret ties to the site, Faye joins the kitchen crew so she can spy on the enigmatic project. When she hears Relic's desperate plan, she has a decision to make...

Armed with a full box of toothpicks (and a little dynamite), can the unlikely trio monkey-wrench the corrupt land deal and recast the fate of Raptor Canyon?

"A gem of a read…"
— Dirk Cussler, #1 New York Times best-selling author

"[You'll be] holding your heart and your breath at the same time…"
— Peter Greene, award winning author of The Adventures of Jonathan Moore series

"A hoot of an adventure novel…"
— Reader's Favorite, Five Star Review.

Grand Master Adventure Writer's Finalist Award

Screencraft Cinematic Book Contest Semi-finalist

Buy now from a bookstore near you or amazon.com

"A RETURN OF THE MYSTERIOUS HERMIT RELIC... A PAGE-TURNING THRILLER" - DIRK CUSSLER
A.W. BALDWIN
WINGS OVER GHOST CREEK
ADVENTURE WRITERS AWARD WINNING AUTHOR
ADVENTURE WRITERS COMPETITION FINALIST 2020
A RELIC NOVEL

A moonshining hermit.
A reluctant pilot.
A $5million plunder.

Owen discovers a murdered corpse at a college-run archeological dig in the Utah outback but when he and a park service pilot try to reach the sheriff for help, their plane is shot from the sky. Owen must ditch the aircraft in the Colorado River, where he is saved by a gin-brewing recluse named Relic. The offbeat pair flee from the sniper and circle back to warn the students but not everyone there is who they seem... The two must trek through rugged canyon country, unravel a baffling mystery, and foil a remarkable form of thievery. Suzy, a student at the dig, helps spearhead their escape but the unique team of crooks has a surprise for them…

Can they uncover the truth and escape an archeology field class that hides assassins and dealers in black-market treasure?

"A beautifully written thriller."
— ***Readers' Favorite Five Star Review***

"[A] humorous, fun, and well-plotted adventure. Baldwin is a master storyteller…"

– Landon Beach, Bestselling Author of The Sail

"Baldwin delivers another gripping Relic tale with trademark wit and deft expression. This is adventure with philosophy that keeps you nodding your head long after you've put the book down."

– Jacob P. Avila, Cave Diver, Grand Master Adventure Writers Award Winner

Wings offers "…action-packed adventure and nerve-racking suspense, with a touch of romance and humor mixed in." Baldwin has a "gift for capturing the reader's attention at the beginning and keeping them spellbound"

– Onlinebookclub.org review

Grand Master Adventure Writer's Finalist Award
Buy now from a bookstore near you or amazon.com

A.W. BALDWIN

DIAMONDS OF DEVIL'S TAIL

ADVENTURE WRITERS
AWARD WINNING AUTHOR

A *RELIC* NOVEL

A moonshining hermit.
An English major.
A $4 million jewel heist.

When diamonds appear in a remote canyon stream, whitewater rafters and artifact thieves set off in a deadly race to the source.

Brayden, an aspiring writer, works in a Chicago insurance firm with his ambitious uncle when they embark on a wilderness whitewater adventure. On a remote hike, they find their colleague, Dylan, dead in the sand, a handful of gems in his fist. When thieves charge in, Brayden flees deeper into the canyon, where he encounters a gin-brewing recluse named Relic. Brayden's uncle is cornered and cuts a deal with the thieves, but they each have a surprise for the other... and the rafters have ideas of their own about getting rich quick... Brayden and Relic must become allies, traverse the harsh desert, and beat the thieves to the hidden gems. Brayden must confront his uncle about suspicious payments at their insurance firm and what he was really doing at the stream where Dylan was killed...

Can they discover the truth, find the lost jewels,

and protect the rafters from grenade-tossing thieves?

"…an adeptly written thriller…the excitement and tension are superb…the entire plot [is] compelling"
— *Readers' Favorite Five Star Review*

"straightforward and thrilling, with humor inter-mixed…Relic is a unique and intriguing character…passionately interested in preserving the ancient archeological sites and conserving the land and water…[We] enthusiastically recommend it to readers who enjoy thrillers, action-packed adventure, and crime novels."
— *Onlinebookclub.org four out of four Star Review*

"Another rollicking Relic ride from A.W. Baldwin…a bunch of double-crossing, dirt dealing, diamond thieves run into Relic's trademark wit and ingenuity. Enjoy!"
— *Jacob P. Avila, Cave Diver, Grand Master Adventure Writers Award Winner*

Buy now from a bookstore near you or amazon.com

"HEART STOPPING EXCITEMENT" – READERS' FAVORITE
A.W. BALDWIN
BROKEN INN
ADVENTURE WRITERS
AWARD WINNING AUTHOR
A RELIC NOVEL

A moonshining hermit.
A budding reporter.
A $25 million misdirection.

The mob, undercover agents, and secret payloads make Broken Inn a dangerous place for a fresh reporter, a newspaper photographer, and a moonshining hermit.

Hailey witnesses a murder at the enigmatic Broken Inn, but when she learns that the hotel manager and her editor are pals, she investigates on her own. When a corrupt guard finds her snooping, she flees into a box canyon, where she is saved by a gin-brewing recluse named Relic. She reports the murder to a deputy, but for some reason, no arrests are made... She enlists help from Ash, the newspaper's photographer, but they must flee for their lives into the back country with Relic and a four-legged stray with a nose for trouble. They discover mysterious metal drums hidden deep in an abandoned uranium mine, but can't tell what's inside. And just when they're most desperate for help, they learn that not everyone is who they seem…

Can they uncover the secrets of Broken Inn, dodge the syndicate, and head off an environmental disaster?

"Danger scorches in another outstanding mystery by A.W. Baldwin"

– New York Times #1 Bestselling author
Dirk Cussler

"Brilliantly executed… heart stopping excitement"
– Readers' Favorite Five Star Review

Grand Master Adventure Writer's Finalist Award

**New York City Big Book Award
– Distinguished Favorite**

Global Book Awards

Independent Press Award – Distinguished Favorite

Books Shelf Award – Second Place

Buy now from a bookstore near you or amazon.com

"A true delight" - DIRK CUSSLER
A.W. BALDWIN
THE ANTIDOTE
LITERARY TITAN
BOOK AWARD
GRANDMASTER AWARD WINNER

Can genetically modified seeds provide the antidote for climate change?

A geneticist has developed plants that could stem the tide of climate change, but when grad student Lila finds him murdered, she flees the scene with the seeds. To escape the killer, she hitches a ride with an eccentric duo and a secret payload that could land them all in prison. Chased by ruthless thieves, the three must rely on their wits, uncover the mystery of these potent plants, and deliver the future of the planet to an unknown scientist a thousand miles away…

But the cross-hairs on those million-dollar seeds are on them, too…

"This harrowing techno-thriller is an impressive achievement – timely, and rich with research, intrigue, and a main character you will be rooting for from the beginning all the way to the exhilarating climax. Highly recommended!"
— **#1 Amazon Best-selling author Landon Beach (The Wreck, Narrator).**

"The chemistry between Harry and Keaton is electrifying." "…there is never a dull moment…The Antidote [is] a gripping novel."
— Readers' Favorite 5 Star Reviews.

"Baldwin is one of the preeminent authors in the adventure-thriller genre and he showcases that talent in spades with his latest novel, The Antidote. A unique premise, richly drawn characters, and constantly increasing risk makes this science-gone-wrong, Crichton-esque thriller a slam dunk. Readers will delight in the protagonists deftly navigating a tangle of intrigue and mortal threats, surviving assassins and gunfights to ensure a brilliant discovery—one that could impact the future of the planet—isn't lost to corrupt special interests and greed."
— Award-winning author Nate Granzow (Get Idiota, Cogar's Revenge).

First Place, Grand Master Adventure Writer's Award
Books Shelf Award - Compelling Read
Independent Press Award -- Distinguished Favorite
ScreenCraft Cinematic Book Finalist Award

Buy now from a bookstore near you or amazon.com

"VIBRANT CHARACTERS... WITTY DIALOGUE AND HUMOR" – READERS' FAVORITE
A.W. BALDWIN
MOONSHINE MESA
ADVENTURE WRITERS
AWARD WINNING AUTHOR
READERS' FAVORITE
BOOK AWARD WINNER
A RELIC NOVEL

A moonshining hermit.
An aspiring lawyer.
A $55 million-dollar eco-scam.

Criminal clients, a pollution mitigation scam, and a million-dollar double-cross make Moonshine Mesa a dangerous place for an aspiring lawyer, an intrepid deputy, and a moonshining hermit.

Something is killing bees, crows, and humans at Moonshine Mesa. When Parker finds suspicious readings at a remote pump station, clients of a prestigious law firm prepare to toss him off a cliff. A gin-brewing recluse named Relic saves him and together they must solve the mysterious deaths, outmaneuver armed drug runners, and rescue an intrepid deputy dedicated to solving the crimes. And all is not what it seems between the partners in these lethal schemes…

Can they unravel these baffling deaths and stem the environmental carnage?

"…a sleuth murder mystery, crime-drama thriller, and action novel all rolled into one page-turner."

"witty dialogue and humor…[with] vibrant characters whose personalities leap off the pages."

"If you enjoy crime capers, dry humor, and quirky characters, you won't go wrong with Moonshine Mesa."

"packs a mighty punch…an action and suspense story that paces itself at a near sprint." Readers' Favorite Five Star Reviews

— Readers' Favorite Five Star Reviews

Gold Medal Award, Reader's Favorite
Gold Medal, Global Book Award
Gold Medal, Literary Titan Award

"...a captivating story filled with suspense and action"
- READERS' FAVORITE
AGAINST THE WIND
READERS' FAVORITE
FIVE STARS
A.W. BALDWIN

The skies are a dangerous place for a teenage pilot with a stolen airplane and a physicist with a quantum computer secret.

Chloe flees her unsafe foster home in a stolen antique airplane. Dochauser eludes a Russian spy willing to kill for the professor's breakthrough in quantum computing. When their paths collide, they begin a cross-country quest to find Chloe's grandfather and a safe haven for the prototype. The Russian mafia, FBI, and social services race to find the runaway and the quantum advance that can tip the balance of world power.

But not everyone in the chase is who they seem…

"…a perfect spell-binding book…The writing was absolutely stunning."
— ***Onlinebookclub.org Five Star Review.***

"…a powerful reminder of the positive impact that human relationships can have on our lives…a captivating story filled with suspense and action."
— ***Readers' Favorite Five Star Reviews.***

"An exhilarating adventure from the opening salvo, 'Against the Wind' follows a global race for next-generation quantum computing technology replete with
hitmen, spies, scientists, and a headstrong runaway
orphan…"

*— Award Winning Author Nate Granzow (Get
Idiota, Black Cordite- White Snow)*

Distinguished Favorite, Independent Press Award

Buy now from a bookstore near you or amazon.com